Also by Peter Anastas

Glooskap's Children: Encounters with the Penobscot Indians of Maine

When Gloucester was Gloucester: Toward an Oral History of the City (with Peter Parsons)

Landscape with Boy: A Novella

Siva Dancing (memoir)

Maximus to Gloucester: The Letters and Poems of Charles Olson to the Editor of the Gloucester Daily Times, 1962-1969

At the Cut: Growing Up in Gloucester, Massachusetts in the 1940s (memoir)

Broken Trip

by Peter Anastas

Copyright ©2004 by Peter Anastas

All rights reserved.

This novel is a work of fiction. Names, characters, places, and incidents either are the product of the author's imagination or are used fictitiously. Any resemblance to actual persons, living or dead, events, or locales, is entirely coincidental.

Printed in the U.S.A.

Published by GLAD DAY BOOKS
P.O. Box 699
Enfield, NH 03748
1-888-874-6904 toll free

Library of Congress Cataloging in Publication Data:

ISBN 1-930180-11-X

Photographs by Ernest Morin
Design by Barbara J. Jones

Contents

Welfare	1
The Snow Man	11
Getting Straight	41
Carly	55
Fatherhood	85
Checks	109
Kelly and Marie	127
Skag	165
The Psych Unit	189
Broken Trip	229

Broken Trip

by Peter Anastas

What ends
Is that.
        Even companionship
Ending.

'I want to ask if you remember
When we were happy! As tho all travels

Ended untold, all embarkations
Foundered.

                        —George Oppen

Welfare

Tony had just booted up his computer when he heard shouting from the reception area, followed by a crash.

"Fuckin' bitch!"

More scuffling, and then a persistent pounding as if the person shouting were smashing a fist against the window of the receptionist's station.

"You act like it's comin' out of your own pocket."

Realizing that only he and Cheri were at work that early, Tony jumped up and headed for the front of the agency.

A big, blond woman in high-heeled boots and a tan miniskirt was slamming her handbag against the Plexiglas that separated the receptionist from those seeking help. She continued to scream at Cheri, who cowered behind the protective shield with its tiny circular window, like the opening in a ticket seller's booth. In the waiting area two wooden chairs with upholstered seats lay on their sides, along with a pile of magazines that had been knocked off an end table. Pamphlets announcing changes in Welfare policies were scattered on the faded green wall-to-wall carpet.

"What's going on?" Tony asked, as the blond woman turned to confront him.

"All's I did was ask for food stamps and the bitch told me I wasn't eligible!" she yelled. "Me and my son are livin' in the car. I ain't workin'. What else does she need to know?"

The woman looked imploringly at Tony. Her hands shook. The mascara around her eyes was running down her face.

"I tried to explain the new regulations to her." Cheri's voice was muffled by the Plexiglas. "If a child under eighteen isn't in school, the unit's not eligible for services—"

"Does that mean he's not supposed to *eat?*" the woman retorted.

Recognizing Brenda as an old client, Tony reached out gently to take hold of her arm.

"Come in the office and we'll talk."

Brenda shook herself free from Tony's grasp.

"What's the point of it?"

"I want to hear your side of the story."

"Don't soft-soap me!"

"Suit yourself," Tony said, as he led Brenda through the labyrinth of cubicles that ended at his office.

Once he'd settled her in a chair next to his desk, Tony handed Brenda a Kleenex. As she dabbed at her cheeks, he noticed that between her boot tops and suede skirt, pulled tightly now against her muscular thighs, her black stockings had run. Under the mask of thick makeup and an apparent splash of perfume, she smelled of perspiration.

"It's been almost a year since we got burned out," Brenda began abruptly. "Once the firefighters left, the neighbors broke through the yellow tape. By the time we got back into the apartment, they'd even ripped off my baby pitchers!"

"Where'd you stay after the fire?" Tony asked.

"The Red Cross put us up a couple of nights. Then we crashed with friends."

"What about Timmy's father? Is there any chance he could help you pay for an apartment?"

"Chasing that son of a bitch down for money is like running after the wind!"

"How have you been eating?"

"We go to the soup kitchen. Once in a while my mother feeds us. But she's in assisted living so we can't stay with her."

"Have you considered public housing?"

"I applied. All's they did was put us on a waiting list. I even went to the mayor to see if we could get bumped up. Motherfucker told me to get a job. How can I work when I got no place to take a shower?"

Just as abruptly as she had begun, Brenda turned suddenly silent. Hands that had been clenching and unclenching lay still now in her lap, the blood red polish of her nails chipped and worn down to the bare nail. The morning sun, slanting across the outer harbor, shed its light on her face.

Tony remembered when Brenda had come to him as a pregnant teenager, her flaxen hair in a ponytail. She'd dropped out of high school to become a carpenter. The first thing he noticed was her capable hands. As soon as she started to show, her boss fired her. Once the baby was born, she went to work on the night maintenance crew in a fish plant, while her mother watched Timmy.

As she sat in the sun, the light playing over her remarkable hair, Tony thought of Brenda's father, who'd been lost at sea. Not long after Timmy was born, her older brother disappeared, washed overboard during a storm. With roots in Nova Scotia, her family had fished out of Gloucester for generations.

As if she'd read his thoughts, Brenda said:

"My people made this town and I can't even get help."

Tony watched as the look of anger on her face changed to one of dejection.

"What's the point of these rules?" she asked. "I thought Welfare was supposed to help people when they were down. I paid taxes when I worked. Ain't I entitled to something back?"

"You are," Tony replied. "The question is how to satisfy the regulations so you and Timmy can have your food stamps. First, let's get you a legal address. Then I think we can ask Timmy's principal to write the Department an 'under the circumstances' letter. If a kid is homeless, how can he get to school? *Where's* he coming to school from, if you get my drift."

Once they'd completed the paperwork together and Tony had called the community action agency to get Brenda and Timmy some emergency food vouchers, Brenda's face brightened.

"How come I had to go through the third degree with that receptionist?"

Tony leaned back in his swivel chair.

"Don't be too hard on Cheri. The poor kid's just doing

what the Department tells her to do. I think the new regulations are excessive. But that's the atmosphere we're operating in."

"It sounds like they want to punish people like me. Hey, I didn't burn that house down! I've never asked for anything I didn't need! Why should I have to beg for help?"

"You shouldn't," Tony said. "And I'm sorry the regulations make you feel that way."

"You're smart, you went to college. What the hell are you doin' in this shit hole?"

"You know I'm not allowed to get personal with clients."

"Gimme a break! How many years have we known each other?"

Tony chuckled.

"Do you want the long answer or the short one?"

"Just tell me the truth," Brenda said. "You were always straight with me."

"I never intended to become a case worker," Tony said.

"You're still working at the college, aren't you? I remember you talked to me once about taking some night classes."

"I teach one course a semester," Tony said. "When Donna and I came back home, I couldn't find a full-time teaching position, so I took the exam for this job. I figured I'd learn something. I thought I might even be able to do some good."

"Fat chance." Brenda laughed. "What's your wife think of all this?"

"We're divorced," Tony said. "Donna's left town."

"So what's holding *you?*"

"With the pressure on the industry I wouldn't dream of leaving."

"Tell me about it." Brenda broke in. "Our dads would be turning over in their graves if they knew the government only gave them eighty-five days a year to fish!"

"I remember your father. Your people were the bedrock."

Brenda looked Tony squarely in the face.

"We ain't any longer. After the fire no one even tried to understand what Timmy and me'd been through. When I told the mayor our building was loaded with code violations, he said it was too late to do anything, I should just get on with my life. That's fine for him, sitting in a big office with the city paying for his own personal Cherokee. I practically had to sell my ass to keep that shitcan of mine on the road!"

"I've got an idea," Tony said. "If you'd be willing to go into a family shelter, you'll get top priority for housing. You might even be able to get a subsidy."

"Do you know what a kid goes through in high school if they find out he's homeless? Gettin' caught at the soup kitchen is bad enough, but a *shelter?*"

"You may have to reconsider," Tony said.

Brenda sighed.

"Timmy's gonna have a shit fit, but I'm desperate enough to put any kind of roof over our heads. I wanna work. There's contractors out there begging me."

Tony leaned forward.

"I know of a program where you'd feel at home. Timmy could go to school each day, you could work. They'd help with housing. The next thing you know you've got an apartment and your life is back on track."

"It sounds too good to be true," Brenda said.

"It won't be easy, but it's worth a try."

Tony wrote down the relevant telephone numbers.

"Ask for Sister Anne Marie" he said. "Tell her we're working together. Once you've made the contact, let me know what happens. Then I think we should send you to Legal Services to get some regular child support."

"You're a peach," Brenda said, grabbing her handbag off the floor. "I'm sorry I lost it. Not gettin' those food stamps was the last straw."

Tony accompanied her through the office that had by now filled up with the other workers.

"I'm gonna stop and apologize to Cheri on the way out," Brenda said.

Then she turned, hugging Tony impulsively.

"Thanks. I mean it."

Tony watched Brenda through the front window as she made her way across the parking lot to a sun-bleached navy Crown Victoria whose fender skirts were pocked with rust. The back seat of the old Ford was stuffed with clothes and sleeping bags. On the rear bumper was a frayed sticker with a Rebel flag on it.

At his desk again, Tony looked at the harbor stretching out behind him, its surface mirror smooth in the airless morning. He pictured Brenda driving away in her battered car. It was unthinkable that no one had offered counseling to her and Timmy after the loss of everything they owned.

The mayor's insensitivity was nothing new. This was the same mayor who told the Boston Globe that the fishing industry was dead and the fishermen had better suck it up. Still, the Board of Health was bound by law to uphold sanitary code rules that called for the regular inspection of rental properties. If the landlord was found to be negligent, there was a chance that Brenda and Timmy might recover some of their losses. Tony made a note to follow up with Legal Services. But he knew from experience that few would have Brenda's interests at heart. For all her turmoil, she had once been a hopeful person. How often had she carried Timmy into Tony's office, proudly showing off her son in his miniature Red Sox ball cap? Recalling Brenda's ebullience, he smiled at the way she'd confronted him about his own life. Maybe he'd said too much in response. He'd been taught that it was unprofessional for a social worker to personalize the client relationship. Yet Tony knew a great deal about the people he worked with. Was it so unethical to share a few simple facts about his own life?

Though it caught him off guard, Brenda's question was valid. Looking back on the rich harvests of his childhood, who could have foreseen a time of few fish? And who could have predicted that instead of being a fisherman, Tony would become a case worker trying to help those who were prevented from going to sea by regulations that were killing the industry he'd grown up in? More painfully, who could have warned him that marriage to his high school sweetheart would fail, or that the academic career he'd seemed on the threshold of realizing would ultimately elude his grasp?

Just around the corner from this office, Tony had once sat on his back porch in summertime, reading *The Bounty Trilogy*. On hot afternoons he'd wandered down the Boulevard to lie on the granite riprap that lined the Blynman Canal. There, in the coolness of the river wind, he daydreamed, while fishing vessels returned from the banks loaded to the gunnels. Tony remembered how desperate he'd been as a boy to find words for all the things he felt, stories that would help him understand a family he seemed estranged from, a life at sea that both attracted and repelled him. Fleetingly, Tony pictured himself then, as he returned to the monitor in front of him to begin the day's work. Cheri had been nice enough to hold his calls while he tried to help Brenda. Now he would have to make up for that indulgence and the stolen moment of introspection it prompted.

It was his day for intake and he knew the waiting room would begin to fill up with fishermen who couldn't work or their wives who wanted help paying the rent. There would be homeless people, like Brenda, who needed a leg up; drug addicts who'd hit bottom, battered women with no place to turn. Tony would sit and listen to their stories, poured out or told haltingly; and from those stories, infinitely varied, often excruciating, would emerge the life of a city fighting for survival.

◇

The Snow Man

The cops gunned down Rochelle's father when she was twelve years old. A month later she found her baby brother blue-faced in his bassinet. After Matty's crib death, her mother, always a chipper, started doing heroin big time. Then she took up with this total loser. Roy walked around the house with his dork hanging out of a pair of Donald Duck boxer shorts. When Rochelle told Denise she thought it was sick, her mother said, "Hey, if you don't like it here, go live with your grandmother."

Rochelle locked herself in her room. She prayed to God to take her so that she could be with her father. Sonny didn't always live with them, but he had been the best dad in the world. He bought Rochelle high tops and he paid for dancing lessons at Miss Tina's School for Ballet and Tap. When Sonny picked Rochelle up after class in his black Trans Am, they rode around town where everybody could see them. Usually they ended up at McDonald's. Sometimes they even went up the line to Burger King. Kids whose fathers lived at home didn't get to do things like that, or ride on a motorcycle.

Sonny had an old low rider. Until he ditched the customized Harley one night in Lynn, Rochelle used to ride on the back with her arms tight around his waist.

Then they'd go like the wind. Her hair blew out behind her and she felt so much older. Sonny treated her that way, too.

But all that changed after he died. Up till then her mother worked as a cashier in the Cape Ann Laundromat. On the days she didn't go to Miss Tina's Rochelle would come over after school and help out. She'd clean the lint screens in the dryers or fold clothes for the customers who requested valet service. Sometimes Sonny would drop in to see them both. If he and Denise were getting along, they'd kiss a little. It didn't embarrass Rochelle to see her parents making out behind the cash register. Denise looked cool in her black leggings and baggy pink cotton sweater. Lots of people thought she and Rochelle were sisters and that made Rochelle proud. Denise wore her hair long, too.

As for Sonny, he was one sharp dude. When he was fighting—he was a solid middle-weight who held the North Shore title for five years—the women couldn't wait to see him box in Salem. Then he started using again. He was dealing to keep up his habit. He lost that suntanned look. The last time Rochelle saw him alive, his complexion looked like cement and his eyes didn't sparkle anymore. But he was still gentle with her, and when Denise wasn't looking he'd slip a couple of bucks into Rochelle's hand.

Rochelle never forgot the night the news came he'd been killed. She was up in her room doing homework when the cops knocked on the back door. They asked for Denise. When Rochelle told them she was over at her mother's, they left without a word. About a half hour later Rochelle's cousin Danny came over and got her. When she arrived at her grandmother's, she found Denise on the floor screaming. Her grandmother was holding her down. Rochelle thought they were fighting until she heard her mother yelling Sonny's name.

An off-duty cop had spotted Sonny driving on Maplewood Avenue. There was a bench warrant out for his arrest. The charge was no big deal, default on a court appearance. But the cop chased him in his own car while he radioed the station. After that, two squad cars converged on the scene with blue lights flashing. Sonny left his car and ran into the woods by the railroad tracks. One of the cops pursued him, firing his service revolver. He later claimed that Sonny had fired on him and he'd retaliated in self-defense. Sonny took two shots in the back. The one that pierced his heart killed him.

The cops produced the gun they said Sonny had fired. It had partial fingerprints on it. The family's lawyer Jack Micheline argued that the gun had been planted on him. Some people claimed to have seen it at the station. They said it was confiscated property. Besides, Sonny had never owned a gun. He didn't even hunt.

Jack sued for wrongful death on behalf of Rochelle and Denise. When the case went to trial, the police testified that Sonny had fired the weapon. It didn't matter that the cop who shot Sonny had wounded someone else a couple of years before, a kid who hadn't even committed a crime. It was the family's word against the department's. Her grandmother didn't want Rochelle to go to court, but Denise and Jack decided she was old enough. Besides, Jack wanted the jury to see that Sonny's murder had left real people behind.

It didn't do any good. The counsel for the police produced records that showed Denise had gotten two restraining orders against Sonny. He demonstrated that the apartments they'd lived in were in Denise's name and that Sonny had done time in Billerica and Middleton. So much for the image of a happy family devastated by Sonny's death.

That was when Rochelle tried to kill herself. She heard at school that you could die from an overdose of aspirin. One night she swallowed a whole bottle, washing the pills down with Diet Pepsi. Denise heard Rochelle moaning in the bathroom. She called the ambulance and they rushed her to the hospital. It was like the night Sonny died, when she had to go with her mother to the morgue to identify his body. The place had smelled like an old refrigerator and it was cold. She wasn't supposed to be there, but the attendant knew her grandmother and persuaded the cops to let her see her father for the last time.

Sonny didn't look dead. It almost seemed like his color had come back. Maybe that was because the morgue was dark. He was lying on a slab in the middle of the floor, covered with a sheet. When they pulled the sheet back for Rochelle to see him there wasn't any blood. But the look on his face was so agonized that she would never forget it. For the funeral they put make-up on Sonny's face and dressed him in his best black suit with a green shirt and a purple necktie, the one Rochelle always hated. He seemed to have shrunk since she'd seen him in the morgue.

All she remembered after that was the people crying. There were so many mourners at the wake, her aunts and her cousins, and the neighbors from when they lived in the Park with her grandmother. Even her classmates were allowed. Sonny's friends came, too; and when they'd all filed past the casket, some kneeling and crossing themselves, Rochelle caught sight of the detective who was always knocking on their door. He stood in the hallway outside the visiting room, looking at the people who'd come to see Sonny. It seemed like he was trying to memorize their faces. Now she knew why so many of Sonny's friends hated the cops.

After they had pumped out her stomach and she was resting, her mother sat holding her hand.

"I promise I'll be a better mother."

Rochelle thought Denise had always been a good mother. She wanted to tell her that, but she couldn't open her mouth. All she could do was make a sound like a baby crying, and that made Denise even sadder.

After the hospital discharged Rochelle and she was back in school, Denise took her to see a shrink. He asked her if she felt responsible for her father's death. His beard was flecked with gray and he had a quiet voice. He seemed nice, but she'd already decided not to answer any questions. Instead, she found herself telling him that Sonny had been on his way to visit her the night he was killed. He was bringing money so she could get her costume for the recital at Miss Tina's.

"If he wasn't coming for me he wouldn't be dead

now," she told him.

"But you didn't kill him, Rochelle," the doctor said.

"I feel like I did." Her eyes filled up.

He held both of her hands. Then he handed her a Kleenex. Blowing her nose made her feel better.

"No one is that powerful, Rochelle. We just don't cause the deaths of people we love. A bullet did that, and you didn't fire that bullet."

"Sometimes I wish I was dead," she said.

"We all do when we lose someone close."

She liked talking to him. After several visits he told her to call him Ed.

"You're a very healthy person, you know. I've seen your school records. You're a wonderful student."

"I like to study," Rochelle said. "Except that it's tough to concentrate now."

"Your teachers understand that. I don't think they'll be hard on you."

"I don't need special attention!" she snapped back, startled at the anger in her own voice.

"I didn't mean that," Ed said.

"I can't stand it when people look at me. I just want to disappear."

For weeks she saw Ed on Wednesday afternoons. She and Denise took a taxi to his office at the Mental Health Center and Denise waited outside. Sometimes Ed asked Denise to come in and all three of them talked. They talked about Rochelle and Denise and they talked about Roy. Denise admitted that Roy was useless except that he went out fishing from time to time. Usually he was so high that he couldn't keep a site. If he wasn't high, he was strung out. Rochelle said that she hated Roy, he brought the whole family down. Denise said she needed him. With Sonny dead they needed Roy's income.

"He's not the best, but he's in my life," she said.

A month later Denise told everyone that she was pregnant.

"I had the test," she said, "and it looks like I'm gonna have a baby."

They had just finished eating supper at Dot's. The TV was going in the background and Rochelle was clearing the table. When Dot said she'd better get an abortion, Denise hit the ceiling.

"I already lost one baby. I ain't killing another!"

"Don't say ain't," Rochelle yelled from the kitchen where she was scraping the plates into the garbage disposal.

"Since when are you telling me how to talk?"

"It's got no class," Rochelle said, coming back into the room. "Just like you and your junkie friends."

Denise jumped up.

"I could slap the shit out of you!" she shouted, lunging at Rochelle, who put her hands up to her face.

Her mother came between them.

"Will you quit it, the two of you," Dot said, holding Rochelle in her arms. Then Denise came over and held her too. Rochelle stood there shaking.

"I didn't mean it," Denise said. She started smoothing Rochelle's hair, its silky texture so much like her own.

The next day Denise went down to the Welfare. She

saw Tony and applied for AFDC for her and the baby and Medicaid for Rochelle. They all went on food stamps. Rochelle had already started collecting Sonny's death benefits, which came to Denise, but there was no medical for any of them. It was the first time in her life that Denise had asked for anything. She never even had fuel assistance. Tony advised her to apply for Section 8. When they were leaving the Housing Authority, Denise started to cry.

"I grew up in the Park. The last thing I want to do is go back there."

"Ma, the lady said it would help pay for our rent at the apartment."

"It might as well be public housing," Denise said. "Sonny would turn over in his grave if he knew we were doing it."

"Sonny's dead," her mother said that night. "It's just you two with another one coming."

Denise didn't say anything. Rochelle knew that her grandmother figured Denise was using again, that's why she couldn't work.

When it came time to have the baby, Roy looked for every excuse to pick a fight with Denise. Dinner wasn't hot enough, he hated macaroni and cheese.

"For Chrissakes, when are we gonna eat real food?" he'd yell across the table. Rochelle could smell the booze on his breath.

"You earn the money and I'll buy you steak," Denise shouted back.

"Fuck you!" he said, getting up.

He came home later and later each night, and then he

just disappeared. One night Rochelle heard her mother screaming in the bedroom. She called 911 and they took Denise to the hospital in the ambulance. They let her stay with Denise in the delivery room. The obstetrician was the same doctor who brought Rochelle into the world. He made her put on a gown and they covered up her hair with a plastic cap. She stood watching while Denise gave birth. She had never seen so much blood. The doctor told her to hold her mother's hand. They all breathed and counted together. Denise quieted down and concentrated.

"That's the way," the doctor said. "Push now, push down hard."

Then the baby came. It was big. At first Rochelle couldn't see whether it was a boy or a girl.

"You've got a beautiful daughter here," the doctor said, as he held the baby up for Denise to see. Denise looked at the baby, but her eyes were really on Rochelle.

"I love you," she said.

At first the doctor was worried that the baby might have been born drug dependent, but tests showed it was okay. Denise went into withdrawal immediately. They had to give her something to keep her quiet. A couple of days later she promised the doctor she would go on the methadone program. The doctor made it a condition of not filing a report with the Department of Social Services, but he warned her.

"I think the world of you Denise, but I'm not sending a baby home under those conditions."

True to her word, Denise went to the methadone clinic. They gave her detox credit for the three-day hospital stay. After Rochelle left for school each morning Denise took the baby over to Dot's. Then she went down to give the urines and take her drink. Once Rochelle was home from school and could watch her baby sister, Denise went to group or saw her own counselor at the clinic.

When Roy finally showed up, he didn't like the idea of Denise going on methadone.

"You weren't here when your own daughter was born," she said. "Now you're trying to keep me from taking care of her."

Roy just walked out of the room.

"Motherfucker!" Denise yelled.

Roy came back and hit her with his fist so hard she fell down.

"You son of a bitch!" Denise screamed at Roy.

The baby, on the couch in her little carrier, started crying. When Rochelle heard the commotion, she ran in to find her mother on the floor. There was blood on her face.

Rochelle grabbed the baby and ran into the kitchen. Still holding her sister, she dialed the police. When Roy came through the door, she had already put the phone down.

"You little rat," he said, coming toward her.

Rochelle dodged the blow he aimed at her, slammed the kitchen door and ran down the stairs with the baby. She was on the sidewalk when the police came.

They arrested Roy. Then they advised Denise to seek a restraining order.

Rochelle urged her mother to do it.

Denise agonized over the decision, finally deciding

against it. She said she would talk with her counselor. Maybe together they could convince Roy to come into the program.

The counselor told Denise to get the restraining order.

"Are you going to wait until he kills you or the baby?" she said.

Denise slammed out of the clinic. When she got home she was high. Roy came back that night. Rochelle could hear them together in her mother's room. Her mother was moaning and Roy was saying, "Atta baby, atta baby. Isn't this better? Isn't this better now?"

They were still in bed when Rochelle left for school. She gave the baby her bottle. Then she took her over to her grandmother's. When Dot opened the door, she just shook her head.

Denise and Roy were high all the time now. There was no food in the refrigerator and no one knew where the welfare checks went. When Rochelle came home from school, the place was a shit house. Sometimes there were junkies lounging on the couch, watching cable TV, drinking beer, wine, whatever was in the pantry.

Rochelle told Ed. He called DSS and a worker was at the house the next day to make an evaluation. They cut off Denise's welfare. They placed Rochelle and the baby at her grandmother's. Rochelle's check from Sonny came to her, too. With the kids out of the house, the Housing Authority stopped the Section 8 payments to the landlord. Dot got a restraining order against Denise. But it didn't make any difference. She and Roy disappeared. One night they moved out of the house, leaving most of the furniture behind. Dot went over and got the TV for Rochelle.

Still, Rochelle did well in school. In ninth grade she got a Sawyer Medal for high academic achievement, and she entered the college course at Gloucester High School. She studied hard and her teachers liked her. Just the same, she missed her mother. Word on the street was that Denise and Roy had split up and Denise was in treatment in Worcester. Before that they'd been in a shelter in Cambridge. Missing her mother, she thought about Sonny. She missed it when all three of them had been together. She couldn't remember how it was when her baby brother was alive because he had died so young. Now she took care of her sister Tiffany. The minute she got home from school she took the baby out in her stroller. Pretty soon Tiffany wasn't a baby any more. She could walk and talk and the sound of her little feet running on the hard wood floor at their grandmother's house made Rochelle want to cry.

High school came and went. During her senior year Rochelle decided to go to nursing school. She really wanted to be a doctor, but even with scholarships she knew there was no way they could afford college. Besides, who would take care of Tiffany? Her guidance counselor said she could go for a BS in nursing at Salem State. It was a full-time program, but they couldn't even afford the transportation. So she decided she would work for a while and go to school at night. She could take some community college courses at the high school extension.

While her classmates went off to college, Rochelle started working on fish. She took the day shift from six to two-thirty at Gorton's Seafood Center so she could be home when Tiffany came back from school. At the Center, where Dot had worked until her legs gave out, they put Rochelle on the packing line. Day after day she took the breaded and cooked fillets of haddock and cod that came out of the fryers and lined them up in cardboard cartons to be quick frozen. After work she helped Dot get dinner and then she walked to school. If she had to work overtime, she only had a few minutes to run home and shower. Sometimes she wondered if she smelled of fish in the classroom or if it was just her imagination.

She took Comp. 1 and World History the first semester and got A's in both. Second semester she took Intro to Lit and Psych 1. Her literature teacher Tony Russo had the class reading short stories. There was one by Alice Munro about a woman who imagines that a man had sex with her on a train. How come English in high school hadn't been this interesting? Then they started reading poetry. Rochelle wrote one of her essays on "The Snow Man," by Wallace Stevens. She loved that poem. From the minute she started reading it, she thought she knew what it was about. No question, Stevens was talking about death. "Nothing that is not there and the nothing that is" had to be about the void that death brings.

Once she started writing she thought about Sonny. She thought about Sonny and she thought about her baby brother. She thought about her mother, too—God only knew where Denise was. She wondered what it was like for Sonny, gone now, and little Matty who hadn't even lived. Although she had to stick to the text, she started writing about how the poem made her feel. She wrote about losing her father and her baby brother. Her paper was longer than the assigned word limit, but she just went on and on. As she wrote she felt better, the way she used to feel when she talked with Ed, her shrink.

When the essay came back, she saw that Tony had given her an A plus. After class he told her that her essay had brought him close to tears.

"Of course you get Stevens," Tony said. "But I loved it that you weren't afraid to write about what the poem drew out of you. That's really what literature is all about."

She said she liked Wallace Stevens. When they read him in high school, she always seemed to know what he was talking about.

"You've got a great aptitude for analysis—and you're such a good writer," Tony said.

Rochelle told him that she wanted to be a nurse.

"Go to school full-time," he said. "The financial aide office in Beverly should be able to help you find the money."

"But I got responsibilities," Rochelle said.

"If you went days for another year and a half you could transfer to Salem. Think about it."

Rochelle promised she would, but she'd already made up her mind that Tiffany came first. Her grandmother was getting older and hadn't been feeling well. Every time she went down cellar to do the wash she came back upstairs out of breath. Denise's disappearance had really affected her. Dot had always been able to keep her feelings to herself. Now she sat in front of the TV with tears in her eyes, watching shows that weren't even sad.

Rochelle kept working. She took more classes, biology and anatomy and physiology. Her lab partner in bio was a kid who'd been a couple of years ahead of her in high school. Larry had always seemed shy in school, keeping pretty much to himself. As they worked on their experiments, he began to open up a little. He told Rochelle he'd been in the service, stationed in Germany. He worked days as a bank teller in Salem, but he was thinking about getting into computers. When Rochelle told him she wanted to be a nurse, Larry said he thought she'd be great taking care of people.

"How do you know?" Rochelle said.

"I remember everybody in school talking about you and your baby sister."

"What did they say?"

"They said you were like a mother to her," Larry said.

"You look like you wanted to tell me something else," Rochelle said.

"You didn't seem to go out with anybody then."

"Hey, neither did you," said Rochelle.

"I couldn't find the right person."

Larry sat across the lab table from her. He was wearing a white shirt and a red and brown paisley tie. His tan poplin pants were pressed. In high school he'd worn his hair down over his ears. Now it was cut close to the sides of his head and he kept it short on top.

During break Larry asked her for coffee. In the cafeteria Rochelle realized it was the first time she had ever sat alone with a guy. She could smell his cologne. Sometimes during mugup at work she talked with the men, but she'd never had a date before. The guys at work teased her about it. Usually she blew them off with some wisecrack. Deep down, though, she wondered what it was like to go out on a date with a boy. In high school it had never occurred to her to go to proms or even to a rock concert at St. Peter's Club or the Legion. She had been too preoccupied with Tiffany and her grandmother. Sitting there with Larry it seemed that a whole piece of her life had passed her by.

"What are you thinking about?" Larry said.

"You're the first guy I've ever had a face to face talk with."

"We could see a movie sometime," he said.

Rochelle didn't dare tell him that she had never been to the movies.

"Why don't I pick you up Saturday," Larry said. "After the show we could maybe go for pizza."

How could she leave her sister? Then she realized Tiffany would be perfectly fine with Dot.

"I suppose so," she said.

"Well, yes or no?" Larry said.

Rochelle laughed.

"Yes, I guess."

After the movie Larry took her to Papa-Razzi at Liberty Tree Mall in Danvers. Rochelle couldn't help staring at the other women. They had such short skirts on! Some sat at the bar with their dates, smoking and talking. They were sipping these big red and green drinks with fruit on top. The overhead lights reflected off the black and white tile floor and the voices rose in the big room. For a minute Rochelle lost track of where she was and who she was with. She felt like she was back in the movie, in a place both new and strangely familiar. There were pictures on the walls of movie stars and other celebrities. Some of them she knew from TV. But it wasn't the pictures that gave her that eerie feeling, or the shimmering tiles on the floor, the waitresses in tight black pants and white blouses. It was like this was the way the restaurant had to be, otherwise people wouldn't think it was real. She wanted to tell Larry what she was thinking, but she figured he'd think she was crazy, or naive, some idiot who'd never been up the line before.

Larry was telling her about the other job he had, working weekends at the Universe Gym in Salem.

"You'd love it," he said. "There's women who work out right along side of the men."

"Work out?"

"Yeah, they pump iron."

"What do you mean?"

"You know, lift weights."

"Heavy ones?"

"Some press forty, fifty-five pounds after just a couple months practice. Hey, let's go tomorrow," he said.

"On Sunday?"

"You don't go to church, do you?"

"Are you kidding?" Rochelle said.

The pizza came on a stainless steel platter. It didn't look anything like Papa Gino's. The crust was thin and there were real tomatoes on it, along with the artichokes they

had ordered and even shrimp.
"This smells delicious," Rochelle said.
"So, are you having a good time?" Larry asked.
Rochelle was quiet for a minute.
"Yeah," she said. "I'm having a great time."

The next day Larry took her to the gym. He taught Rochelle how to use the exercise machines, and while he worked out she sat in on an aerobics class. There were guys there, too, exercising just like the women. Pretty soon they had a routine. Saturdays they'd go out to a movie or for some supper. Then on Sunday Larry would pick Rochelle up and they'd go to the gym. Larry told her she looked beautiful in her electric blue lycra tights.
"You're a natural," he said.
"Cut it out!"
"I'm not kidding," he said, as they sat at the health bar drinking protein shakes.
Rochelle could feel herself blushing.
"No one's ever told you you're good looking?"
"Yeah once," Rochelle said. "My Dad used to."
"I knew Sonny."
"You knew my father?"
"I used to see him fight."
For the first time Larry put his hand over hers. Her immediate impulse was to pull away, but she just left her hand under his.
"You must miss him," Larry said.
"I think about him all the time."
Larry leaned toward her. With his fingertips he

touched her face.

"You're so pretty," he said.

The first time they went to Larry's apartment in Beverly Rochelle was nervous. It was small but she saw right away how neat he kept it. Usually they watched TV, but once Rochelle made dinner for them. After she'd set the baked scrod on the table and they were sitting across from each other, she shivered. Larry opened a bottle of white wine and they had a toast. It was the first time she'd ever tasted wine. She liked its coolness on her tongue, the way it felt going down. But the shivering feeling stayed throughout the meal. It was as if she were meant to be there with Larry. She wanted to tell that to him, but she didn't know how to say it. She wasn't sure what the feeling meant. My God, she thought, is this what love is?

What she felt for Larry was different from what she felt for Dot or when Tiffany came in from school. That twinge in your chest when someone so familiar suddenly enters your field of vision and you feel connected to them. It comes from living together, from knowing their little quirks. The way Dot cleared her throat before she expressed something that was hard to say. Or Tiffany's habit of looking down almost with shame before she asked Rochelle to buy her something she was dying to have.

She felt that twinge in her heart for Larry, but it came less from knowing him well than from wanting to know him better, from wanting him to know her. Sitting across the table from each other and eating the meal she prepared for them, drinking a little of the wine in the stemmed glass, was what she desired more than anything else. She hadn't realized she was lonely before she met him, before they started spending so much time together; but now she understood what it had been like without Larry and she realized, even in the midst of working or helping Tiffany with her math, or shopping at the Cape Ann Market with Dot, what a terribly lonely time it had been. She'd felt lonely after her father died and her mother disappeared. Now it came to her that she'd been that way from the very beginning and she didn't want to be that way ever again.

Rochelle knew that she and Larry would make love soon. She knew it because she wanted to feel closer to Larry. Even though she had never been close to a boy or hardly ever thought about sex, she had read about it in novels and actually seen people do it in the adult movies on cable TV. After nights of just kissing and touching they began slowly to undress each other. Lying on Larry's bed naked, it seemed right, even urgent, that they make love.

Rochelle wasn't afraid. Larry had told her about a girl in Germany he thought he was in love with. Solemnly he said that they had made love and it had been his first time. And after he told Rochelle she held him, pressing herself close to his chest.

"I don't mind," she said. "You didn't know me then. Besides, I'm glad you know more than I do."

Larry was gentle and didn't rush and she loved it when he was inside her. Then she was on top of him and moving and it felt fantastic. Their bodies moved against each other like they moved in the gym and she enjoyed the way you tightened your muscles and then let go.

"I never knew I had a body until I met you," she told Larry as he drove her home.

"I like the way you talk," was all he said.

Late that night the police knocked on the door, waking Rochelle. Denise's body had been discovered at an abandoned warehouse in Lawrence. They identified her from the food stamp card in her pocket. She'd been dead a long time. It looked like she had crawled into the warehouse after shooting up. She froze to death, the medical examiner told Rochelle. He said there wasn't much left of her mother to see.

They buried her at Beechbrook, next to their grandfather. Welfare paid for part of the funeral. The rest came out of what Rochelle had saved. Dot's minister tried to do well by Rochelle and Tiffany at the graveside service, but he really didn't know them. And what could he say about a woman who had abandoned her children, dying alone in an old factory? At least that's how Rochelle thought about it as she stood next to Larry, who kept his arm around her. After the service he came back to the house. Dot liked him a lot and Larry made a special effort to sit next to her on the couch.

Rochelle expected that Denise's death would put an end to that part of her life, like the period after a sentence. She figured she could get on with things like going to school and taking care of her little sister, seeing Larry. But it didn't turn out that way. She found it harder to get out of bed in the morning and she hated going to work.

She hated the filth that came out of the mouths of the people at the plant, especially the women. They all knew she was seeing Larry.

"Have you fucked yet?" they'd ask her, or "When are you two tying the knot?"

She thought about talking to Ed. But when she called the hospital to ask for an appointment, they told her that the state had terminated the funding for his position. They offered to place Rochelle on a waiting list for one of the social workers, but the thought of starting from scratch, of telling someone she didn't know about everything that had happened, seemed overwhelming, so she put it off.

One afternoon Tiffany came home early from school and found Dot lying back in her chair. The TV was going and Dot wouldn't wake up. Then Rochelle came in and touched her grandmother's face, her hands. They were cold. When the ambulance came, they said that Dot had died of heart failure. This time the funeral took all of Dot's insurance. The minister came to visit a couple of times, but Rochelle had nothing to tell him aside from reassuring him that she would take good care of Tiffany. After Rochelle left for work, one of the neighbors would see to it that her sister got off to school. And when she came home, Tiffany would have just come in the door. During the two nights a week Rochelle was in class, she hired a baby sitter. Things were tight without Dot's check, but then Tiffany's death benefits from Denise started coming. That paid for the sitter.

One night after Tiffany had gone to bed, Rochelle

was doing the dishes when she heard a noise behind her. She turned to find Roy standing in the middle of the living room.

"Where's my baby," he said.

"Who are you talking about?" Rochelle heard her voice shake.

"I came to see my daughter."

"Tiffany's asleep."

Rochelle could smell the booze on Roy. Should she call Larry or the police? When Roy saw her eyes dart toward the telephone, he grabbed her arm.

"It's late," Rochelle said, trying to shake free of Roy's grip. "She's got school tomorrow."

Roy wasn't listening.

"Don't shit *me!* I'm her father and I'm gonna see her right now."

He was staring at her breasts.

"Hey, Rochelle, you're all grown up. You look just like your mother."

"Get out of this house!" she said.

"Now let's just have a little talk," Roy said. "You sit down here and we'll see who's who and what's what."

Rochelle turned toward the kitchen. Maybe she could get out the back door and wake the neighbors before Roy got to Tiffany upstairs. But Roy thrust his face up close to hers. Shouting for help, Rochelle pushed him away.

"You're a tough little bitch," he said, squeezing her shoulders.

Rochelle broke away from him and ran into the kitchen. She pulled the bread knife out of the drying rack.

When he came toward her, she held it up in front of her. Roy went for her hand, but she stabbed him. The knife punctured his throat. She jabbed it in harder. The blood rushed out all over her hand and she heard Roy choking. He fell forward. It sounded like he was trying to catch his breath. The blood was pumping out of his neck. It pooled on the floor under him. Rochelle stood there with the knife in her hand. When the cops came she was still standing over Roy's body.

A grand jury inquest found that Rochelle had acted in self defense. The police testified on her behalf, citing numerous restraining orders against Roy and his criminal record: drug dealing, breaking and entry, receipt of stolen property, assault. Still, Rochelle felt that she'd committed a crime. She had killed her sister's father, no matter what she thought about Roy or what he might have done to her or Tiffany. The DA explained to Rochelle that she was under no obligation to Roy. He wasn't even registered as Tiffany's father.

"Think of yourself as saving your sister's life," he said. "Your own, too. You're a brave person. A lot of people admire you for what you did."

Rochelle didn't feel that way. She couldn't let go of the image of Roy's blood pumping out of the hole in his throat or the terrible gurgling sound he made. Beneath that, though, she'd really wanted to kill Roy for what he had done to Denise and Tiffany, for coming into their lives and spoiling everything after Sonny had died. But she didn't tell anybody how she felt. Just feeling it frightened her.

Larry came and sat with her. At first she didn't want to

talk, then she didn't want Larry to say anything. Finally she didn't want Larry to be there at all.

One morning Rochelle woke up vomiting. She hadn't even thought about her period since Denise's body was discovered. She must be pregnant. In all the confusion she'd probably forgotten to take one of her birth-control pills. When she came home from the family planning clinic and told Larry she was pregnant, he wanted them to get married right away. He'd just been offered a job in New Hampshire.

"I'll work," he said excitedly. "You'll be able to go to college full-time. We'll find a town with a great school for Tiffany. We can be a family!"

Rochelle looked blankly at Larry.

"I really love you," Larry said. "I thought you loved me."

Rochelle just shook her head.

"I can't love anybody," she said.

Larry's new job was in software sales. He found a condo rental in Durham and he got ready to move.

"Let's go, let's go," Tiffany said on his last night. She hugged Larry, she tried to hold her mother's hand. But Rochelle just sat there until Larry got up to leave.

"No one's telling you to carry all that weight by yourself," he said as he left.

Rochelle decided to work until just before the baby came. Then she would go on welfare. School was out of the question. She dragged herself to the plant each day and came home every afternoon for Tiffany. Tiffany was now almost the same age she had been when Sonny died.

Rochelle looked at her long dark hair with the red highlights in it, at her little body getting rounder, her sturdy legs. Twice a week Tiffany went to Miss Tina's and she loved her dancing lessons. Rochelle tried to be upbeat with her sister. Once the dishes were cleared and washed each night, she sat down to help Tiffany with her homework. Tiffany was quick and bright, the way Rochelle had been, but there was a sadness about her. There were times when Rochelle looked across the dinner table to find Tiffany far away. What would become of her with all that loss?

At night, after Tiffany was in bed, Rochelle sat up watching TV. To keep from thinking about Larry, sometimes she read, or tried to read. Once, even, she got out her old Lit textbook. Looking idly through it she found "The Snow Man" and read the poem again, remembering the paper she had written. It was filed away in the bottom of her clothes closet with the rest of her college papers. She read it sitting on the cold floor of her bedroom; and she read her teacher Tony's comments, which had seemed to praise her too much.

But she looked at the poem again, and when she read it she thought that she hadn't got the meaning right. It wasn't a poem about death, as she had believed, or the cold, empty feeling of loss that death brings. It wasn't about death at all. The poem was about how you came to understand any reality, whether it was frost, pine-trees, leaves, the cold, even suffering. You have to feel it yourself before you can know it, Stevens seemed to be saying. You have to "have a mind of winter" before you can inhabit the cold and the wind "that is blowing in the same bare place." You have to be both the "nothing that is not there and the nothing that is."

When Rochelle went to apply for welfare, Tony was on the intake desk. He recognized her immediately and that put her at ease. In answer to the required questions about paternity, Rochelle told Tony about Larry. Tony said he remembered him from the night classes.

"You're not together?" he asked.

Suddenly sounds from deep inside her came out and she couldn't stop them. Tony got up from behind the desk. He came to her side and put his arm around her.

"I'm so embarrassed," she said.

Tony rummaged in his desk and came up with a paper napkin.

"It's all I've got," he said.

Wiping her nose Rochelle thanked him.

"Then it's not cut and dried," Tony said. "I mean with Larry."

"I loved him," Rochelle said. "I love him. I'm just—"

"It's been too much, hasn't it? And losing your grandmother on top of it all. Did you think about seeing anybody? I remember you wrote a paper once about your therapist."

"He's gone," Rochelle said.

"And you didn't want to talk with anyone else?"

"I couldn't get it together."

Tony sat back on his desk.

"I know what you mean," he said.

Then he suggested she could get AFDC for herself and

the baby. She would qualify for Medicaid and food stamps and still keep Tiffany's survivor's benefits.

"It's not a lot," he said, "but it will help until you decide what the next step will be. At least it will pay for the baby."

When Tony had mentioned the baby, who was due now in three months, Rochelle broke down again. Finally, when they finished all the paper work and Tony had made a list of the documents he needed to activate her case, Rochelle got up to leave.

"Rochelle," Tony said looking into her eyes. "You were such a good student."

It was eleven o'clock. There was no sound from the street, only the silence of the house around her. "The nothing that is not there and the nothing that is," she thought. Talking with Tony had broken the dam inside of her. She had promised him that she would call the hospital the next day and make an appointment. In a way she looked forward to the relief of it. It wouldn't be with Ed, but she was just a girl when she'd begun seeing him. She was Tiffany's age, and now she was old enough to go to therapy on her own. She *was* on her own and she had been for some time. The thought was comforting. It's okay, she thought. I really know how to be by myself. But there was another need. It was like the need she had once felt to write out her thoughts and feelings for Tony's class each week. Only this time it was the need to talk with someone close, not just a counselor or a therapist.

It was late, she should be in bed for work the next day. Still, she got up and went to the telephone. Carrying it back to her chair, she put the phone down in her lap and dialed the number Larry had written on a slip of paper before he left. She dialed the number and heard it ring.

Getting Straight

"Keep smoking like that you'll end up with cancer."

"Hey, at my age you were shooting up!"

"When I was sixteen I didn't know any better."

"Just stay off my case, Ma. I don't live with you no more."

"You know I'm working to get you back. I been clean for a whole year."

"Big fucking deal!"

"Where'd you get that attitude?"

"D'you ever look at yourself in the mirror?"

"My fucking Jesus! Will you quit being so mean?"

"If you don't like what I say keep your trap shut!"

"Knock it off, will you?"

"I'm outta here!"

When Doc got home from group, all the lights were out. He found Jade curled up on the couch in the dark. It was only a week since she'd bought it at the Salvation Army thrift store so her daughter could sleep over.

"I bet Crystal was here," he said.

Jade's voice sounded like it came from far away.

"What did I do to make her so fucking angry? Just tell me that."

Doc and Jade were junkies. The staff at the methadone clinic liked to call them "recovering addicts," but they knew better. They had sniffed shit and injected it; they'd taken it in speed balls and they had shoved it up their asses. Doc dealt and Jade shoplifted. They had done time and now they were trying to get straight. Each morning at 7:30 they went down to the clinic for their daily dose. They gave their urines and they took the methadone dissolved in cranberry juice that the nurse brought out in little white paper cups. After dosing, the other junkies lingered on Main Street swapping war stories. Doc and Jade went directly home if they didn't have counseling or group.

Crystal wasn't Doc's daughter. That son of a bitch was six feet under. Jerry came home from Vietnam with a habit no VA hospital could get him to kick. He ended up ODing on the train from Lynn, where he went to score.

After she had Crystal, Jade went back to live with her mother. Her father died at sea when she was ten. A storm capsized the dragger he was fishing on. A few years later her mother remarried. But Jade couldn't stand her stepfather. Jake owned a bar and it seemed like every chance he got he had his hands all over her. When Jade took up with Doc she moved out. After they were busted, the state gave Crystal to Mary. That's where she was now, pending a custody hearing.

Doc got his nickname because he had a talent for forging scripts. Working in hospitals as an OR tech, every chance he got he'd rip off a resident's prescription pad and write for his buddies. Percs, Dilaudid, he knew the

PDR by heart. He even prescribed for sick friends. If they didn't get better, at least they got high.

Doc and Jade had been back together for a year now. They wrote to each other from the slammer. When Jade got out she took a one-bedroom unit on Chestnut Street so Doc would have something to come home to. Their combined income on disability was a little over a thousand a month. Five-fifty came off the top for rent. Another hundred covered the utilities, leaving them a bill a week to live on. Even though it was stuck away in the basement, Jade had fixed the apartment up with second-hand furniture and some things Mary gave her from the house. Mary still came over. At least Jade and her mother got along.

Doc sat down next to Jade and lit up.

"You know we should quit," Jade said.

"My counselor says one habit at a time."

Doc had on a "Just Say No" T-shirt and his graying hair was slicked back. It made his nose look more hawk-like. Now that he wasn't using he had put on weight and he was a lot calmer. Jade, whose mother had named her for her green eyes, was usually hyper. She tried quitting coffee, she exercised, she even went to yoga class at the clinic. Just the same, she was wired.

After her Narcanon meeting at St. Ann's that night, Jade stopped to get coffee at Dunkin' Donuts. Usually she took it home, but she decided to sit at the counter and go over what she'd heard in the church basement.

Looking out at the plaza, Jade saw a bunch of teenagers smoking and talking. In the glow of the mercury vapor lamps their faces seemed like purple masks. Through the window she saw each person's mouth opening like in a movie without sound. Somehow all their actions seemed slowed down. Among them she saw a pretty girl with red hair and long legs. She was wearing cutoffs. Between the fingers of her left hand she held a cigarette and she seemed to be doing most of the talking.

Jade sat watching her daughter as though she was observing her own behavior, the way she had once waved her hands and pushed her auburn hair back with a flick of her fingertips. A couple of older guys came up. One stood with his hands on his hips, a key chain dangling from his belt. They looked like truckers. They wore skin tight jeans and T-shirts that showed their guts.

"Beer," Jade thought. "And dope."

She wanted to shout out to Crystal to wise up. Instead, she imagined herself out there. She remembered how it was when you were high and you didn't give a shit what happened or who said what. She remembered when you had to cop and nothing got in the way of it. Didn't make a difference if it was parents or friends. She remembered what it was like to hold the syringe. After you cooked up you found a line and hit it. Pretty soon all your craziness began to go mute and everything went cool inside. The feeling came over you that nothing could touch you. You were immune from pain, from insults and humiliation. You were in your own world and nobody could hassle you.

The next day she told her counselor what she'd felt.
"I just wonder what the payoff is staying straight."
Julie looked at her.

"If you weren't straight you wouldn't have these insights."

"But who needs *insights?*"

On Julie's wall there was a map of New Mexico. It looked like it had been torn out of a child's coloring book. There was a circle drawn around Santa Fe in purple ink and another farther up around Taos. A jagged red line connected the two points.

Jade didn't even know where New Mexico was. She had never been good at geography. She hadn't been good at much of anything in school. At sixteen she dropped out and went to work on fish. A year later she was pregnant with Crystal. After Jerry died she was constantly high. She did whatever she needed to do in order to stay that way. And she never looked back. She fucked her brains out and now she couldn't get off.

"I can't come anymore," she told Julie. "I can't have an orgasm with Doc. I can't even have one with myself!"

"Did it ever occur to you that you might be angry?" Julie asked.

"Angry? I'm bullshit!"

"Well, don't you think the anger holds you back?"

"I never used to be this way. When I was using I was always mellow. I was laid back and I liked it that way."

Julie crossed her legs. She was wearing a long rust-colored Indian patterned skirt and sandals. Her short blond hair looked bright yellow under the fluorescent lights on the ceiling. The desk was cluttered with papers.

"So what's the difference now?"

"There ain't none."

"You sure?"

"Yeah, well, my head's clearer."

"Isn't that something?"

Mary came over after supper that night. She and Jade sat smoking and talking in front of the TV. There was some dogshit sitcom on, but Jade was too involved to grab the remote and turn the fucking tube off.

"She's gonna drop out," Mary was saying.

"And you can't make her stay in?"

"Did you ever do what I wanted you to do?"

In the lingering light she looked at the lines of worry in her mother's face. She had put some of those creases there, she knew, and now Crystal was doing the same thing.

"Julie says we should see the principal," Jade said.

"I been already. Once she's sixteen they can't keep her in class. Anyways, Crystal told me last night she wants to work and get her own place."

"Her own place?"

"You did it," Mary said, getting up. "You wonder why my hair's turning gray."

Jade hugged her mother.

"I love you, Ma. No one asked you to take her in but you did."

"Don't forget, I tried to give you a home, too."

Jade walked Mary to the door.

"You gave me a home," she said. "I just didn't know how good it was."

Before group one night Mary called.

"Crystal's disappeared," she said.

"What, Ma?"

"We had a fight last night and she never came home."

"You sure she's not staying with a friend?" Jade asked.

"I called everybody. No one's seen her."

"Oh my sweet Jesus!"

When Jade started screaming into the phone, Doc came in from the kitchen.

"She's gone," Jade shouted. "My baby's gone."

The police put out an all points on Crystal. They called the FBI in, figuring as a runaway she might have crossed state borders. Three or four days went by with no response. Jade lay on the couch, the telephone on the floor beside her. Mary was in and out.

At midnight the phone woke Jade up on the couch. The call came from a women's shelter in Fort Worth. They had Crystal. Once she learned that Crystal was okay, Jade was too emotional to talk.

"She hitched a ride down on some truck," the worker whose name was Delores told Doc. "When the driver found out she was only sixteen, he tried to send her back home. That's when she ran away. One of our people found her outside the Greyhound terminal."

"Oh my God she was raped!" Jade shouted once Doc put the receiver down.

"It doesn't appear that way."

Doc sat on the couch and put his arms around Jade. He held her tight as she sobbed.

The next morning Doc left for Texas. With Mary's help they scraped up his plane fare and the cost of Crystal's ticket home. Doc wanted Jade to come, too. But unlike Doc, who had spent three years in the Air Force, she'd never been on a plane before. Besides, she couldn't go a day without her methadone even though Julie said they'd give her take-homes. Leaving for the train station to Boston, Doc looked handsome in a Hawaiian shirt and khakis, his extra clothes in an Adidas workout bag.

Jade stayed awake for two days and two nights waiting for them to arrive. When they finally came through the door, Crystal looked like she'd been on vacation. She was wearing a long, loose-fitting flower print dress and a big straw hat. Doc had bought them for her in Texas.

"Hi, Ma," she said, as Jade hugged her, crying her heart out.

"D'you know you nearly drove your grandmother and me nuts?"

Crystal's tears were wet on her mother's face.

"I just had to go somewheres. But when I was on the road all's I wanted to do was come home."

The day after he got home Doc had trouble getting out of bed. He blamed the fatigue on jet lag, but it was more like he had the flu. For weeks he'd been waking up in a cold sweat. He told Jade it was probably a reaction to the lower doses of methadone they were giving him at the clinic.

"We better get you to the doctor," Jade said.

"Naw, just give me a couple aspirin," Doc said.

A few days later Doc was coughing badly.

"Ma, he don't look good," Crystal said when she came over.

"He's running a temperature," Jade said. "But you know him. He's his own doctor."

That night Doc couldn't stop coughing. He was covered with sweat. It came off of him faster than Jade could wipe him down. She called the rescue squad and they rushed him to the hospital in the ambulance.

The next day the doctor told Jade it was pneumonia, but they wanted to do more tests.

"He's never been sick," Jade protested.

"We need to be sure," the doctor said.

A week later the doctor told Jade that while Doc's system seemed to be responding to the antibiotics, his T-cell count was dangerously low.

Jade was very still. She didn't cry, she just sat there.

"Is it what I think you're talking about?" she asked.

"Yes," he said. "But let's just take it one day at a time."

When Doc came home he was weak, but he could sit on the couch and watch TV. He and his counselor had decided that because of what he was taking for his lungs and his immune system he should try detoxing from the methadone. He seemed to be handling it pretty well.

Jade went alone each day to the clinic and she came back after group to sit with Doc. He had asked her to find some medical books for him at the library. He was reading up on HIV disease as though it was somebody else who was infected.

"You knew it all along, didn't you." Jade held Doc's hand.

"The night sweats started in prison."

"How come you didn't tell me?"

"You had enough on your mind with Crystal," Doc said quietly.

After supper Crystal came over.

"Ma, I'm pregnant," she announced.

Jade went ballistic.

"I knew that fucking trucker raped you!"

"I told you he didn't touch me!"

"Then who is it?" Jade screamed. "I don't need this!"

Crystal looked steadily at her mother. On Julie's advice she had been seeing a counselor. Jade noticed that she was much less quick to fly off the handle.

"It's just some stupid kid. We did it once after I came back. I don't know why. It was dumb."

"You been to the doctor?" Jade asked.

"I'm three months along and I ain't gettin' no abortion."

Jade called Mary over and the three women had a talk. There was no question of marrying the father, Crystal barely knew him. Besides, he was seventeen and still in school. Once he graduated, they'd hit him up for child support. Crystal planned to work until the baby came. She would go to night classes to get her GED. Jade said they could attend together.

When Crystal went into the bedroom to tell Doc, he was already asleep. Some days he felt good, other days he could hardly hold his head up. When he talked, his voice was raspy and you could hear the fluid in his lungs.

Then he had another bad turn. After the ambulance had taken him to the hospital again, the immunologist told Jade that pneumocystis carini had set in. There were also purple welts on Doc's skin. From their reading Jade knew the lesions were the first signs of Kaposi's sarcoma. Doc was in the third stage of AIDS.

After her blood screening came back negative, Jade sat talking with Julie.

"Why him and not me?"

"You told me Doc always used a rubber," Julie said.

"He did it so I wouldn't get pregnant."

"It kept you from getting infected, too."

"But he's gonna die," Jade cried to Julie. "And I never even had the chance to love him."

"You're loving him now, aren't you?"

Jade slumped down in the chair. She lit up a cigarette even though she had just told Julie she was trying to quit.

"Not the real way," she said. "I never gave him anything of myself. All we've done is nurse each other. Now this fucking disease takes over!"

"Love is a lot of things," Julie said. "I've watched you with Doc and with Crystal."

Jade and Crystal went to GED classes every night at the library. On the weekends, when Crystal wasn't working at Empire Fish, they studied together. Crystal was really good at math. It was years since Jade had done fractions or long division, but Crystal helped her get the hang of it again. Jade enjoyed English and history; she also discovered she was good at the computer. It got her thinking about job possibilities. The tutors were easy going, and nobody at the Adult Learning Center pushed you or made you feel stupid like they did at Gloucester High. Sometimes when the two women were together they got laughing hysterically over their mistakes.

"Quiet down, you guys," Doc would protest from the bedroom. "School isn't supposed to be fun!"

But Doc was getting worse. All they could do was keep him comfortable, the immunologist said. They were trying a combined therapy of Hivid and Zidovudine to stabilize his blood count, but nothing seemed to work. His T-cells were down under a hundred and he didn't have much pep. Jade would often find him asleep in front of the TV even though he'd just taken a nap. The purple and black welts multiplied all over him, while his skin seemed to darken generally.

Thanksgiving came and Crystal had an ultrasound. She knew the baby was a boy. She told her mother and Mary that she wanted to name him Brandon. That was Doc's real name. She said she wanted it to be a Christmas surprise for Doc.

Doc went to the hospital again and this time they didn't think he would make it. His immune system had collapsed. Exposure to an infection as minor as a head cold would cause a violent reaction. Mary spent every day with Doc. Even Jake, her husband, came at night and they all sat around quietly. Jade decided that Jake wasn't so bad after all. He'd never been much of a talker. Jade sat alone with Doc.

"I'll never love anybody else," she said. "And I won't sleep with anyone again."

"Of course you will."

Doc could barely speak, but he smiled when she pressed his hand.

"You'll find someone to love," he whispered. "I want you to."

After they took him off life support, Doc died peacefully, just the way he wanted to. It was as if he had simply slipped away. Crystal held one hand and Jade the other. Jake and Mary were at the bedside. Doc's counselor Joe stood vigil outside with Julie.

Afterwards, all Jade felt was empty. The house was empty and her heart seemed that way, too. Julie suggested that maybe it was time for Crystal to move back with her mother. The clinic prepared an expedited custody petition for the court and the judge agreed to it. Jake and Mary helped them look for a bigger apartment. Pretty soon they found a nice two-bedroom on Dodge Street, on the backside of Portagee Hill. You could see the entire city from a little sun porch off the kitchen. On a clear day you could look all the way out to Boston.

Jade was on take-homes now. It wouldn't be too long before she'd be completely off methadone. From the windows of the new apartment they could see Gloucester glowing beneath them in the dark, the flashing reds and greens, the electric blues of holiday lights outlining people's houses. Even the fishing boats were illuminated with strings of white lights hanging from the rigging.

Next morning the movers were coming. And the night after would be their first together in the new apartment. As they stood side by side looking out the window, Jade kissed her daughter softly on the cheek. Then she reached down gently to touch her full belly.

"Just think, Ma," Crystal said, putting her own hand over Jade's. "I'm gonna be a mother."

"And *me*, for a change," said Jade.

Carly

It wasn't till he caught her bareass down the Oval, in the front seat of some dickhead's Camaro, that Carly's boyfriend found out she was hooking.

Mike yanked the guy out from behind the steering wheel. He flattened him up against the fender and was just starting to chew him a new asshole when the poor bastard yelled, "Chill out, man. I ain't in love with her. She's makin' me pay for it!"

Mike stood there. He didn't even react when the guy slipped into his car again and gunned the engine. By then Carly had pulled her jeans back on and was buttoning up her blouse. She figured it was her turn now. But Mike seemed frozen in his tracks. Under the streetlight she saw tears running down his face.

"Why did you do it?" was all he could say.

Carly didn't know whether to tell him the truth or not.

"I needed the money," she said. But that was only part of the truth. How could she tell him that she liked picking up guys? She liked the thrill of it. She liked the feeling it gave her to have some jerk creaming his pants over her tush.

"I'd of given you the money," Mike pleaded. "Don't I treat you good?"

"Yeah," Carly said. And she meant it. Mike was decent,

only she didn't need him hanging onto her every mood: "What's the matter? Are you okay? You look sad."

Well, stick that up your cahootie! Sometimes she felt sad. Sometimes she felt like dancing down Rogers Street. Mostly she wanted her freedom, even if it meant doing a stranger once in a while. The gang at the House of Mitch, where she hung out after work at Tasty Sea, knew her secret. Nobody at Mitch's got on her case about it.

Anyway, Mike was from up the line. He worked installing tapedecks at Custom Auto Radio on Route 1. They'd only been going out a couple months. But it was silly to think he wouldn't find out about her little vice, as she liked to call it.

Mike drove her back to her place on Angle Street. She got out half expecting him to say one last hurtful thing, maybe even belt her. She might have felt sorrier if he had whipped her buns. She might even have loved him more. She might have felt closer to him from the beginning if he had been more assertive. Instead, he drove off and she never heard from him again. Last she knew he was back in Peabody living with his mother.

The truth was Carly didn't see herself as a hooker. She'd always worked, even before she dropped out of high school. If a guy turned her on she'd fuck him, period, end of sentence. She was surprised Mike hadn't asked her for it the night they met in Beverly, dancing at Grover's that first time. It wasn't a question of money. She earned enough with all the overtime they got at the plant. Face it, it excited her when somebody offered her money. Not everybody, just guys she liked the looks of. Others she blew off.

Like that fat city councilor who came on to her shitfaced one night at the Bungalow, bawling that his wife wouldn't give it to him anymore. "Get a life," she told him. "And a new wife while you're at it!"

The first time someone had offered her money for sex was when she was twelve. Her mother had this black boyfriend she met at Manny's Lounge, across the street from the Park where the women drank on the nights after their welfare checks came. Once, when Carly was alone with him, Buford offered her ten bucks to suck his cock. She was sitting at the kitchen table doing her math homework when she noticed him standing over her. He had a ten dollar bill in his hand.

"Carly, can you do me something?"

She hadn't said a word when next thing he had his fly open and his cock was out. At first she was surprised. Not to see some guy's dork—she'd been looking at pricks ever since she could remember—but because it was so small. She'd always heard that blacks had the biggest dicks imaginable.

Make a long story short, she sucked him off. She sat there in the kitchen and he told her what to do and she did it. Buford handed her the money and went back to watching the Bruins game. After she got over being surprised at what they'd done, she didn't think it was such a big deal. A couple of weeks later, when he asked to see her naked for twenty bucks, she let him undress her. One thing led to another and she and Buford were fucking. He taught her everything, including how to keep from getting knocked up. Her mother called it rape when she came home one night and found them together in the big bed. By then Carly had started liking it. She liked it so much she found other guys to do it with, only she didn't ask them for money.

Her mother had thrown Buford out. And she told Carly if she caught her screwing around again she'd put her in a home. Carly didn't stop; she just made sure she didn't do it where her mother would catch her. But Carly wasn't the only teen who was having sex. Lots of kids she knew in the Park were screwing. They fucked each other and they fucked their mothers' boyfriends. One girl was pregnant by her own brother, half-brother actually.

After it was over with Mike, Carly took it easy for a while. She worked and she went out drinking with her girlfriends. Most nights they tooled around, pony tails sticking out of the backs of their ball caps. Dressed in Reeboks and *My Heart's in Gloucester* T-shirts, they pulled up along the Boulevard and shot the shit from car to car. There was a lot of dope down there and the cops cruised hourly looking for drug deals. But Carly stayed clear of that scene. Once in a while she'd smoke a joint. But dope didn't do much for her. Neither did booze. She'd have a Bud or two—actually she liked Sam Adams Lite. That was the extent of her drinking.

What Carly really enjoyed was checking everything out. She liked to sit in the back seat of Linda's little white Cabriolet and watch the world go by. Kids she knew in high school and never spoke to again turned out to be junkies with five-bag-a-day habits. Girls she'd grown up with in the Park wheeled carriages with sleeping babies in them while they looked for guys to hit on. One of them, Gloria, who had the biggest tits at GHS, had twins now and her boobs were humungous. Most nights she hung out braless in a fishnet shirt and cutoffs that showed how fat her ass had gotten since she and Carly had sneaked smokes together in the girls' locker room. When her mother wouldn't watch the little boy and his sister, Gloria pushed them down the Boulevard herself in their stroller. Sometimes they slept right there on the sidewalk while Gloria straddled some dude naked in his car. She didn't give a flying fuck who saw her. Once she was so stoned she couldn't push the stroller straight and the kids woke up and started bawling. Gloria just stood there with a dazed look on her face like they were somebody else's babies.

Carly thought about Gloria a lot. Sometimes when the packing line was slow and they were waiting for the next batch of breaded cod fillets, she imagined herself in Gloria's situation, strung out and on welfare with two kids, her red face looking like she had a perpetual sunburn. When she pictured Gloria like that she was glad she'd never been knocked up. She knew that even though she always thought she'd be a mother, she'd get an abortion in a minute if she had to. She didn't want to be saddled with that kind of responsibility—yet. Only too clearly she remembered her mother, having one kid after another until there were no units in the Park big enough for them and they had to be moved into Section 8 housing on Cleveland Street next to Uncle Moe's, in that tenement that smelled of cat piss all the time.

Her mother didn't give a good rat's ass about getting

pregnant. She even seemed to enjoy it.

"Now you tell me, Carly. What else have I got but my kids?" Lorraine used to say in the most uncomplaining way.

Nights on the Boulevard, especially the long summer ones, reminded Carly of Fiesta in June, when everybody came out for Greasy Pole and the fireworks. Kids from Saugus and Revere, from all over the North Shore, blew into town. She remembered how it was in high school meeting them all, learning who the latest band was, listening to them rap. It was like a whiff of the city years before a gang of them, dressed to the nines, started taking the train on Sunday afternoons to hit the Boston dance clubs. Sometimes they partied so late at Zanzibar they missed the last train home. Then they'd take a room for the night at the Hotel Manger, right there in North Station. There'd be four or five of them sleeping in two beds, raising hell, shouting out the windows, tossing tampons down on the street, until security came by to shut them up.

That's what Carly thought about down the Boulevard while she sat in Linda's Cabriolet and watched everybody milling. It was like Gloucester was the only place to be. It was what she knew and who she knew; and she liked it that she'd go to work every Monday and get her check without fail on Thursday. She paid her rent and utilities on time, not like her mother, facing shut-offs in the middle of the winter or on fuel assistance to save her lazy ass.

Carly paid her bills and she went shopping at the Mall twice a week with Linda, even if it was on a work night. She loved tooling up the line after supper at five with everybody else on the highway. It was like a race, the cars all leaving Grant Circle rotary between five and six. Some people from the plant had supper at 4:30 so they could go right to the Mall and be home in time for Beverly Hills 90210 or Roseanne. Hey, life could be worse, especially when you were working steady. Come winter there'd be the lay-offs. By that time she always had a few dollars put by. Anyways, you got to collect. Which wasn't too bad considering that you could go South between checks, especially now that they mailed the unemployment to you. Some people just stayed in Florida all winter. They had a friend forward their checks to them.

But Carly didn't think much of Florida. Nothing but a bunch of old farts crowding the streets or sitting on benches gobbling Munchkins out of waxed paper bags. If that was paradise she'd rather go to hell.

But one night everything changed. She was leaning against Linda's car when a guy with a tan that wasn't any salon job pulled up behind them in a white Corvette. Carly had never laid eyes on him before. When he got out of the car he was tall and skinny and he had a face like Robert Redford, except that his hair was longer. It was fine and blond and the wind off the water blew it out behind his head. He was wearing 1950s strip sunglasses even though it was just getting dark.

Linda told Carly his name was Chet. A murmur went through the gang when he stood right there in front of everybody and lit up a joint. Chet kept on toking while the cops drove past, slowing down. And after they left nothing registered on his face.

Carly couldn't believe what she was seeing. Pretty soon a few of the guys circled around Chet and they were all passing joints. But Carly just stood there.

"He's done time," Linda said.

"Wherever he was there must of been a sundeck."

"You like him, huh Carly?"

In five minutes Carly had wormed her way into the group around Chet. Two seconds later they were talking. In ten minutes she was waving good-bye to Linda from the Corvette.

All night long they fucked at his parents' cottage on Long Beach. They fucked their brains out and Carly never made it to work, a first for her. When she woke up and saw Chet standing naked in the window looking out at the sun over the ocean, she knew she was up for anything.

No more nights on the Boulevard. Chet would pick her up after work and they'd head out of town. They cruised Marblehead, stopping for a beer and a burger at Jacob Marley's; they hit the Cineplex tearing home back down Route 128. When his parents were in town, a rare event, he stayed with Carly. Mostly she hung out with Chet at Long Beach, trucking into work with circles under her eyes and a tingle between her legs, just in time to punch in.

Chet told her what he'd been in the joint for. A little B&E was all, receipt of stolen property; nothing earth-shaking. He still saw his parole officer, but that would be up in a couple months. Right now he worked prepping cars at his father's Budget Car Rental franchise in Woburn.

Basically, they cruised and they hung, that is, when they

weren't in the sack, which was a hell of a lot. Carly told Chet about her secret life. He compared it to his own habit of breaking into people's houses.

"I like the risk of it," Chet said. "The money's cool, too. But the taste of danger in your mouth—that's the cat's ass."

Carly had never felt so close to a guy. Chet let her take care of him. She grilled steaks for him and washed his clothes. And in bed he took it slow and easy like no guy had ever done before. She couldn't get enough of it. When they were together, she had her hands all over his body. When they were apart, all she thought about was his blond hair and his smooth skin.

Her girlfriends teased her.

"When's the wedding?" Linda asked on one of the rare nights they sat down the Boulevard together.

"Hey, when you're getting the best sex of your life who's keeping count?"

One night when they were driving home through Beverly Farms Carly asked Chet if he'd ever been in one of those big estates.

"You want me to tell you the truth?"

"'Course I do!"

"My first big job was right here. Piece of cake. Everybody away on vacation. Jewelry up the ying-yang."

"But whad'it look like inside?" Carly said. "Was it pretty?"

"House Beautiful all the way."

"I wish I could see it."

Chet slowed the Corvette down. He put his hand on Carly's thigh. It was a warm summer night and her hair was streaming out behind her in the soft air. Chet's hand felt as cool as the wind.

"You wanna?"

"Wanna what?"

"Do a little sightseeing."

"How?" she said. "When?"

Chet gunned the engine again. As the car picked up speed effortlessly Carly saw him smiling.

"It takes a little planning." His lips closed tightly. "A little research. I'll tell you how."

That night Chet showed Carly a map of the North Shore. He pointed out the locations of the houses they'd been driving past. He told her that you just didn't show up at their front doors expecting to be asked in.

"You case the area first," he explained. "You figure most of these people are on vacation. They've got summer places, or they're off cruising."

"Cruising?"

"Yeah, on their boats."

"Then what?"

Chet took his time, drawing the story out for Carly.

"You pick a likely prospect. You ascertain if any one's home. You can do that by calling up at odd hours. Sometimes it takes a few days. You might even do a little reconnaissance."

"How's that?"

"You pretend you're a delivery person trying to leave a package. You go up to the service entrance and you knock. A maid could answer, anyone. If there's no answer you try the same thing later on, or the next day. You try the front door, too. You keep calling. If there's no answer on the phone or no long beeps on the answering machine; if no one comes to the door, there's a good chance they're all away."

"Then what do you do, break in?"

"That's too quick," Chet explained. "You've got to disarm the security system. First you check the wires. Then you see if there's a loudspeaker for the alarm on the house that you can reach by climbing the roof. Sometimes you need a ladder."

"But how can we do all that in a Corvette? Besides, someone would notice the color."

"You rent a van," Chet said. "And you carry a ladder on it just like a plumber or a carpenter would. You drive right up to the house, even in daylight."

"I wanna do it with you," Carly said. "I gotta see how you work."

"Hey, not so fast. You realize what happens if something goes wrong?"

"Shit's creek."

"Worse," Chet said. "There's nothing more depressing than the slammer, especially if you're a woman."

Carly jumped up from the couch. Outside Chet's parents' house the waves were crashing.

"But we wouldn't get caught! I know we wouldn't. You're a pro!"

Chet pulled Carly gently down beside him. He turned her face toward him, his blue eyes fixed on her.

"Everybody gets caught," he explained. "You start with that premise, with the knowledge that no matter who you are or how good you are, you're eventually going to get nabbed. It's the risk that drives you, not the fear, and especially not the need for what you're boosting unless you're a junkie or a coke head."

In the following days Chet showed Carly how to pick a likely prospect. He taught her about the importance of isolation, and easy access and exit.

"You gotta be able to get out fast," he said. "To run if you have to."

"You mean, dump the car?"

"Whatever works."

Pretty soon they found a place to hit.

It was a big white house on the Manchester-Beverly line, right on the ocean. There was a driveway in and out and the house hung over the water screened on three sides by trees.

Chet looked the family up in the Voters' List at the Manchester Public Library. The owner had a yacht yard in Marblehead; his wife sold real estate. They were both 55. If they had kids they must have been living out of state because they weren't listed as voters. When Chet called the number that was listed, they got no response, not even an answering machine. They figured the couple must be away on vacation. It was the first week in August. Hey, the guy probably had a boat of his own.

That afternoon Chet drove up to the front door in a black minivan he'd borrowed from his father's lot. He knocked on the door as if he was making a routine call. When no one answered he went around back. Locating the wires for the alarm, he noted the location of the speaker, figuring that he could scale the roof at night without a ladder. He checked the routes in and out of the driveway.

Chet still had the van when he picked Carly up that night. They drove around until 1 a.m., trying the house on a car phone. When they got no answer, they decided to hit it.

Once Chet had disabled the alarm, he forced the lock on a glass-paneled door and they slipped in. Each of them had a flashlight. But Carly wasn't prepared for what she saw. The whole downstairs was one big open space looking out to sea. Even though there were no lights outside the house the moon lit everything up. Soft white light poured in the windows revealing a deck that seemed to wrap around the entire house.

Everywhere she looked there were paintings on the walls. Not those schlocky waterfront paintings that you saw in the banks in Gloucester, but ones like she'd never seen before. Paintings of old hills that looked like photographs. And the furniture was like the stuff in the windows of Adesso in Boston, Italian metal floorlamps and endless white couches. Carly wanted to put the lights on and look at everything, but Chet told her to hurry up, they'd search the bedrooms first.

Upstairs the master bedroom took her breath away. With windows on three sides, the room was so big you could have put five king-size beds in it. The moonlight illuminated everything. Sitting on the bed Carly could see the surface of the ocean, the lights of Eastern Point across the water on the left side of the house and those of Salem off to the right.

"I can't believe this," she shouted to Chet who was going through the dresser. The moonlight reflected in his hair. Getting up off the bed, Carly opened the sliding glass doors onto an upper deck.

"Stay in," Chet said, shining his flashlight into the drawers. "I got the woman's stuff here if you want to see it."

Carly lay back on the bed. A soft breeze blew in from the sea. All around her she smelled perfume and face powder. She luxuriated in the firmness of the bed, the smell of clean bedcovers.

"This beats the Park any day," she said. "Growing up all those years in that shit hole who'd ever think that I'd be in a house like this?"

As Chet came past the bed Carly reached out for his hand.

"Come and see the water. Just lie here for a minute with me."

Chet held her hand.

"This isn't a vacation."

"I don't give a shit about taking anything," Carly said. "All's I want to do is make believe I live here. Let's pull the curtains and put the lights on. Please, just so I can see everything."

"Don't be crazy. Neighbors could catch the light through the trees. If they know these people are away they'd be suspicious something was up."

"Just for a minute, please."

Quickly Chet pulled the drapes across the windows. Then he let Carly turn on a small bedside lamp. The room was enormous with white walls and off-white drapes. On the walls were bird prints and the wall-to-wall carpeting was soft and thick.

"Come and kiss me," Carly said, pulling Chet down to her. "Hold me. It's like a dream with the ocean out there and this bed. I don't ever want to leave."

As Chet bent over her Carly heard a cracking sound. Just then all the lights in the room came on and she noticed Chet's bleeding face as he fell onto her. Screaming, Carly pulled herself out from under his dead weight. Chet's blood gushed over the bed covers. Her arms and legs were sticky with it. As she tried to get up she felt herself slammed on the side of her head by something hard. Now she was on the floor. A man with a terrible blank face stood there hitting her. He was hitting her and shouting at her. She felt the blows digging into her skin, crushing her bones, until she couldn't see or feel anymore.

What happened after that Carly didn't remember. All she knew was what her friends told her as she lay in the IC unit in Beverly Hospital, pain killers insulating her from the horror of the knowledge. Later, at Shaughnessy Rehab in Salem, she tried to make sense of it all. Chet was dead from a single bullet in the brain. She didn't recall how; she couldn't even see his face. All she felt was the space in her life he no longer filled. She felt it like a weight of sadness that never left her, but she couldn't seem to cry about it.

Linda was there every day, and her mother, too. She and her mother hadn't been close in years. But Lorraine's constant presence was a comfort. She helped Carly up and down the corridors in her walker or out to the solarium where she'd sit. The nurses had her up and moving as soon as she came out of the ICU, but without the walker she didn't walk right. She knew that immediately. She couldn't seem to move in her old quick way. It was like she had to turn her entire body to look or put all her weight behind each tentative step.

As for her face, once the bandages were off she scarcely recognized herself. They'd had to shave her head in order to get at the lacerations. But that wasn't half of it, or the dark blue under her eyes that wouldn't go away. One half of her face didn't square with the other, and it looked like a piece of her nose had been sliced off on the side, making her face skinnier. They told her that her nose had been broken along with her cheekbones and jaw.

At first she couldn't talk. Then slowly she began trying to say what she heard in her head. Sometimes it felt like her tongue was too big. Words came to her mind, but she had trouble spitting them out. A speech therapist worked with her twice a day. It was weeks before she could actually have a conversation. And then she knew that something was wrong with her right side.

Slowly what had happened became apparent to her. Linda told her that the judge had arraigned her from a hospital bed. She'd been charged with breaking and entering. There would be a formal hearing and eventually a trial. She also understood that because of what had happened to her and Chet in that house, on that bed, that an inquest was underway. Kevin, her public defender, a young, curly-headed guy who looked more like a lumper than a lawyer, told her that a grand jury was looking into Chet's death. He also told her that Chet's parents had filed a wrongful death suit against the property owner who had shot Chet in the head. Carly would be expected to testify.

Carly's boss Tom came to tell her that she didn't have to worry about hospital bills. Her medical insurance covered everything and the disability income from her benefit package would give her 60% of her salary for the next six months. Linda agreed to deposit the checks when they started coming. She paid the rent on Carly's apartment and she kept up with the utility bills and Carly's Visa card.

Everyday when Carly woke up she dressed in jeans and a top. She began slowly to walk around in her Reeboks. The girls had even brought the Red Sox cap for her to wear. She had her old clothes, her sneakers; her bills were paid and her apartment was ready for her return. She even had her job to go back to. Chet's parents had brought her a photograph of him to keep, but after she looked at it she put it in the drawer of her bedside table. She didn't reach for it again.

They were nice people, Chet's mother and father. She had barely spoken to them when she and Chet first went out; but they had seemed kind then. Now they treated her like part of the family. They said they knew that she and Chet weren't criminals. In the short time they had been together they had seen that Carly had been good for him.

"We know it was a lark," Chet's father said. "We realize Chet didn't do it for the money. You guys weren't even armed."

He sat down next to the bed.

"Sometimes he just did crazy things," Chet's father said. "It was like he needed to find out what it felt like to do them."

Carly didn't know what to say. She couldn't answer because that part of her life was gone from her. It had been obliterated by the blows to her head and face, the blows from the same rifle whose bullet had killed Chet. Chet didn't exist anymore, nor did she as she had known herself. The person she now saw in the mirror was the only person she recognized.

Pretty soon she could get around without a walker. The doctor said she could go home, but she couldn't go to work yet. The neurologist held out hope for some improvement in her walking. She told her that nerves often miraculously regenerated.

"Join the Y," she suggested. "Get as much exercise as you can. You're young. Put all this behind you. You've got your whole life ahead of you."

At home in her sunny little one bedroom apartment on Angle Street she found some comfort. A health aide came to help her with personal care and the physical therapist was there to exercise her leg. Lorraine shopped for her and the two of them talked.

Carly looked at her mother while they sat watching As the World Turns. Lorraine had always been overweight. Carly remembered how she once joked that being big was what attracted those black truckers to her. But there were no more blacks. In fact there were no guys at all. Lorraine was middle-aged now. The children were out of the house.

All she looked forward to now was the time when she could get into elderly housing.

"I'm sorry I was so nasty," Carly told her mother.

"Sweetie, I was mean to you," Lorraine said, reaching out to touch her daughter. "I spent too much time partying. And what have I got to show for it but this?"

Lorraine spread her arms to indicate her bulk.

"Just look at *me*," Carly said as she began to sob.

"Let it all out, honey," Lorraine said. "You got a right to feel bad."

Weeks passed and Carly finally left the house. She limped down to the plant to visit the gang. Everybody was glad to see her again. Even Tom came out of the office and hugged her. Then they told her the bad news. Tasty Sea was shutting down. The new conservation regulations that cut vessel time at sea to eighty-five days a year were taking effect. Landings were down by more than half.

"We can't pay our bills," Tom said. "The investors want me to sell or diversify, but I can't find a buyer in this market. Scratch trying to bring in a new a partner."

By January Carly's sick benefits were exhausted. She was responsible now for the entire premium on her Blue Cross. Reluctantly she walked down to the Welfare on Commercial Street.

Tony helped her apply for temporary disability, which would give her limited medical coverage. She got food stamps and they talked about her getting Social Security Disability payments.

"I really want to work," Carly said.

"But what do you do when the work isn't there?" Tony

asked.

"I grew up on welfare. I promised myself I'd never live that way again."

Tony took his half-glasses off. From across his desk he looked directly at Carly, unlike the people whose eyes slid away once they saw the changes in her face or body.

"I know what you've been through," he said. "Look at it this way. You've worked for years and you've paid your taxes faithfully. Now you need the help you've subsidized for others. Don't be ashamed. Just be glad it's there for you when you need it. The way the governor's heading it might not be around much longer."

Carly had never met Tony before, but she'd heard her mother and her cousin Brenda talk about him for years. He never acted like the money was coming out of his own pocket like some of those other social workers did, treating you like dirt when they took your applications or when, in the old days, they were required to make home visits. Carly even remembered when case workers looked in the closets to see if there were men's clothes there because if you were on AFDC you couldn't have a guy living in the house. There was one bitch, who arrived for your recertification visit in a white El Dorado. She'd come into your kitchen and wipe the seat of the chair off with a handkerchief before sitting down.

"Okay," Carly said. "But as soon as I can work I'm gonna go back."

"You might consider re-training," Tony offered.

"I can't see me in school."

"That was a while ago," Tony said. "You'd be surprised

how many people go back and love it."

On the way out, Carly paused, turning to smile at Tony.

"I almost forgot. I have a message from Brenda. She asked me to thank you. She's working and Timmy's back in school. The shelter found them an apartment."

A week later her case was on the docket. It was a jury trial because her public defender had suggested that she might get more sympathy once a jury heard her whole story.

When it was time for the defense, he put Linda and Tom on the stand first. They told about what a good worker Carly was and how she paid all her bills on time. Thank God nobody asked about the guys she used to pick up! Then it was Carly's turn. Once the jury had seen her injuries and understood the circumstances of her crime, they were liable to go easy on her. Sure she and Chet broke into the house, but they weren't armed and they hadn't taken anything, Kevin stressed. All they did was lie down on the bed. Carly admitted it was wrong to have violated someone's privacy. She said she had pushed Chet into doing it for the excitement.

Still, the jury found her guilty on two counts of felony, breaking and entering and entering at night. The judge gave her a two-year sentence, which he immediately suspended. He told Carly she'd suffered enough, but if she violated her parole she'd be in hot water. For good measure he gave her a hundred and twenty hours of community service to perform.

The night after the trial Carly went down to Mitch's for

the first time since she got out of the hospital. All the old gang was there and everyone welcomed her back. Still, she knew something was missing, like when she visited the plant. People came over and talked to her, but it seemed like they did it out of duty. She noticed how they looked at her out of the sides of their eyes, as if they didn't want to linger on her battered face. And if she got up to move to another table, her friends stared over her head rather than look at the way she dragged her leg a little behind her.

As for hitting it off with any new guys or somebody she'd occasionally shacked up with, Carly felt instinctively that it was no longer a possibility. It wasn't just that she'd lost her looks—Christ, she was skinny as a rail! Who'd be interested in sleeping with her now, not to mention the way her face was scarred? Rather, it was that she didn't want to be the old way anymore. Those urges had gone, and with them all the electricity that sparked when she saw a guy she wanted and knew he wanted her, or she could make him want her. It was all bled out of her, all the pizzazz and heat that used to explode in her gut, making her say and do crazy things, coming on to guys she'd never laid eyes on before. It was gone now and it seemed like everyone around her knew it.

Linda came over and said pretty soon it would be cruising time on the Boulevard. She had a Jeep Ranger now and she promised Carly she'd pick her up and they'd drive around town with the top down. Carly answered "All right!" But when she heard her own voice she knew it sounded fake. She began to count the minutes before she could get away. She looked at the clock above the bar and all she wanted was to be home in her own bed.

Linda picked up on her mood right away. Putting her arm around Carly, she said, "Carly, you had such a mouth on you! Where's all that piss and vinegar gone?"

Carly's eyes dropped.

"I guess they beat it out of me."

"No *suh!*" Linda said, hugging Carly hard.

When she saw her internist the next day, he told her he detected some depression.

Carly just shook her head. And then she started to cry. She cried so hard she thought her throat would split.

"I'm going to prescribe something," the doctor said handing her a Kleenex. "Let's try these pills for a while."

Carly took the anti-depressants he gave her and a pill to help with tension and anxiety. After she'd taken them for a couple of weeks she admitted that she felt better. The only thing was, she felt like she was experiencing the world through a see-through blanket. It was all out there, but it was like everything was soft around her. Not only the things she reached out to touch like a coffee cup, but the voices of the people who came to see her.

Lorraine appeared to her through a fog; and all Carly could do was sit there as if there was a pair of hands pressing on her head, forcing her down into the chair.

One night she sat in front of the TV and she couldn't breathe. She was alone and she got scared. She began softly to moan and cry, she couldn't stop herself. And then she thought about Chet. She thought about Chet for the first time and she started to scream. She screamed so loud the neighbors called the police. When the squad car came, they had Lorraine with them, and all of them went up to the emergency room together.

The next day they transferred Carly to the psych unit at Addison Gilbert. For two weeks she had daily meetings with a counselor and group therapy morning and night. After they changed her meds she started to feel better. Both in therapy and in group they talked about loss. Every woman she was with on the unit had suffered some irreparable loss, it seemed. For one it was her teen-age daughter, raped and strangled after she'd gone out at midnight to a convenience store in Danvers. Another one's husband had OD'd on crack cocaine right in front of her. Several had been abandoned by their husbands or boyfriends.

"Nobody deserves to lose the person they love," was the theme of many of their discussions. The women came to feel that the terrible things that had happened to them didn't occur because they were bad or because they'd brought them on themselves. They learned to separate what happened to them from how they actually experienced it.

Carly spent hours in those groups and she began to feel incredibly close to the other women, some of them old enough to be her mother. Talking together they agreed that one way or another they'd been abused. Carly told them about her need to seduce men.

"Hey, when we feel powerless all's we got is our cunts!" a Puerto Rican woman named Josie shouted.

Everybody laughed and then the room went quiet as each woman turned to her own thoughts.

When it came time to go home, Cary wished she could stay. But her MassHealth only covered a limited amount of in-patient care. She was released to her mother.

One day Carly woke up. It was June and the sun came into her bedroom. On her dresser sat the picture of Chet his parents had given her. In the hospital she had learned that it was better for her to live with that picture, with the memory of Chet and what they had shared, than to deny it, hiding his image where she couldn't see it, where it couldn't cause her pain. That photograph of Chet with his long blond hair and smooth complexion no longer hurt her to look at.

All she felt was a quiet buzzing when she looked at the picture or when she thought about Chet. She felt like she imagined a cat would feel when it was purring softly next to a warm stove or in someone's comfortable lap. She felt like she used to feel in the plant when Tom or one of the foremen was explaining a process and she stood still and listened and the interest became hypnotic, almost as if she was being lulled to sleep.

In fact, the next day Tom came by. He told her he was starting a new business. He was going to smoke mackerel and herring, pack it in Cryovac, and sell it in the U.S. and in Europe. He said there was a big market for gourmet portions of fish. Tom said he wanted Carly to come to work for him.

"Not packing," he said. "I want you to help run my office."

"Me?"

"Yeah, you," Tom said. "I think you'd be great at it."

"But I don't know anything about keeping books."

"You could learn," Tom said. "In fact, there's a computer course starting up next week. You could attend at night, right on Main Street. We'd pay for it."

Once she was out of the house Carly's life took a new turn. She went to work for Tom at 8 in the morning. Linda was in the new business, too, and a lot of the old gang. It was a small shop down on the old FBI wharf, right across from the vacant plant, and they had state-of-the-art smokers. The orders were coming in good, the office manager told Carly. It was Carly's job to answer the phone. She was learning how to do inventory. And the computer course was a breeze. After the basics and Windows 95, they started working on Microsoft Office. Carly found out she could handle everything they taught her. She'd never even thought about data processing before. Now she could even do an Excel spread sheet.

Then it was St. Peter's. It was Fiesta, the third weekend in June. It started with a block dance at St. Peter's Park on Thursday night. The carnival had gone up before she knew it, even though it was right across the street from her house. The entertainment booths were there along with the altar where the statue of the saint of the fishermen was lodged, the statue she'd known ever since she was a little girl when Lorraine had taken her each night, walking from the Park to Main Street and then down the Fort where Fiesta was always held. Everywhere Carly smelled the aroma of sausages and green peppers steaming on a grill, of cotton candy and fried dough dusted with powdered sugar.

Each night Carly joined the gang, first at Mitch's then at the Blackburn Tavern that had just opened again. They listened to the Megawatt Blues Crushers and they danced. Her friends drank too much and they carried on. Carly danced, too, and she had a beer. She liked being part of the gang again. They talked about the new business and about how this Fiesta was so significant because of the strain on the industry, on the whole city's economy, from the new conservation restrictions. Everybody talked about how Fiesta, the celebration of the Italian fishing heritage of the city, was more important than just having a good time.

Carly went to see the Greasy Pole races on Saturday and Sunday afternoons. She watched the men she'd known all her life rush out on the slippery log dressed in crazy costumes, trying to grab the flag at the end of it. She watched Sammy "Stronzo" Gigante win the contest again, and she stood silently while Cardinal Law blessed the fleet as each boat, decked with flowers and bright streamers, sailed past the viewing stand.

"May there always be fishing boats in this harbor," the Cardinal said, as he sprinkled drops of Holy Water onto the decks and riggings of the passing vessels.

At night on Sunday she watched the fireworks from Pavilion Beach; and then, after Fiesta was over and the carnival had shut down, she walked with everybody down the Fort and around the Square. She walked behind the fishermen who had removed St. Peter from the altar, his robes pinned with hundreds of dollar bills.

The procession started out at St. Peter's Park and marched up Commercial Street past the empty fishplants to Fort Square. It was dark and hundreds of people—fishermen and their wives, neighbors, the cops and the firemen, the gang from the plants, tourists even—marched behind the statue of St. Peter that the men carried on their shoulders.

One of the men started the chant Carly had known all her life, even though she wasn't Sicilian. He shouted out, "Viva San Pietro," and another replied, "Viva San Pietro!"

Then someone yelled, "`E che siamo tutti muti?"

"What are we *tongue-tied?*"

Then they all yelled "Viva San Pietro" as loud as they could. And it went on like that for the entire procession:

"Viva San Pietro!"

"`E che siamo tutti muti?"

"VIVA SAN PIETRO!"

"VIVA SAN PIETRO!"

"VIVA SAN PIETRO!"

Through the Square the crowd marched, through the entire Sicilian neighborhood. Women and children leaned out of the windows of the tenements and single family houses, shouting, urging the crowd on. They tossed confetti down on the marching people and they yelled once more:

"VIVA SAN PIETRO!"

Carly had never felt like this before. Even though she'd done the march many times, it never felt this way. All around her were people she knew, or their mothers and fathers. Even their grandparents. It didn't matter that she wasn't Italian. As they returned to the door of St. Peter's Club on Main Street, where the statue would stand in a front window for another year, she started to cry. Carly cried not because she was sad but because she felt the depth of what they'd all experienced together, what they'd desired in wishing eternal life to the saint, who watched over the men in the boats and the sleeping people they left behind at dawn. She cried because for the first time in her life she felt part of everything they had prayed for during the Fiesta. But even more, she felt part of the city she'd grown up in, the city where she worked and where her own life would stand or fall with the lives of everyone else for another year.

It was quiet on Main Street as she walked home alone. The Fiesta lights were out and the altar was dark. The dancers were gone and the drinkers had disappeared. The streets were littered with empty ice cream cups and the crumpled sheets of wax paper they wrapped the fried dough in. Here and there she saw a colored streamer illuminated by the halogen lamps of the street lights. She walked past the Blackburn Tavern up to the filling station. Her leg was dragging the way it did when she got tired, but Carly didn't care. Everyone knew what had happened to her leg, and her face, too, and it didn't bother her anymore. She turned right on Angle Street and there was her apartment. She went in without bothering to put the lights on. All she wanted was a quick wash before getting into bed. Tomorrow was Monday and she had to be at work bright and early.

Fatherhood

It was only a few days before the big ninth grade formal and Terry kept hoping his father wouldn't forget the promise he'd made to spring for a rented tuxedo. That way he could afford a corsage for his girlfriend Dina. Right up until the afternoon of the dance Terry waited for Randy to appear with the money. He'd already put a couple of bucks down on the tux and Dina's corsage had been ordered at Audrey's Flower Shop. But as the hours went by and Randy didn't show, Terry figured it was going to be like all the other times. Randy would promise to come to his birthday party or to his little sister Carmen's. Patiently they'd wait for their father, hoping that Randy might be bringing something special for them. Pretty soon the party would end and their friends would leave. Night would fall and still no Randy. Or he'd come a day late, empty handed: his car broke down, an old friend suddenly appeared, he got busted.

But this time Randy never showed at all. Terry lost the deposit on the tux and Dina's parents were ripshit they'd bought her a hundred dollar gown for nothing. Audrey's even called demanding payment for the corsage. Two days later the cops in Lynn telephoned Terry's mother. Randy's body had been found near Union Square. It looked like he OD'd on the street. Whoever he was shooting up with stuffed him in the dumpster behind Richdale's and split.

When Lorna got off the phone she freaked out. She screamed, grabbing a flower pot to smash the kitchen window. Then she disappeared into her room. Terry found her passed out on the floor. Her works lay beside her, covered with blood. By the time the ambulance got to their second floor apartment on Friend Street, Lorna was already in convulsions.

Neighbors sat with the kids until the DSS worker arrived. She placed Carmen in temporary care. Terry's godmother Annette offered to take him until they released Lorna. But the state worker wasn't keen on keeping Terry and his sister with their mother.

"This is the third time we've had to place these kids," she told Annette crossly.

As it was, Lorna never made the funeral. Annette took the kids to Greely's to get one last look at their father. But the casket was closed and there were no visiting hours. No one remembered what religion Randy had been, so the funeral home asked the auxiliary minister from Trinity Congregational to read a prayer over the grave.

As Rev. Doben fumbled with the words, Terry and Carmen stood on the lip of the grave. City workers waited a few feet away, impatient to begin shoveling the dirt back in. When they got home that night, Carmen said nothing. For three days she was speechless.

Terry stayed with Annette and her two kids. He took the day of the funeral off from school. The next day he hooked, getting Dina to write him a note. Annette's apartment was on Trask Street, on the south side of Portagee

Hill. If you looked out the window what you saw was neighbors' yards with laundry flapping on the lines. Dogs barked day and night, tangled in their own leashes.

Annette was a hot shit. She knew Terry'd skipped school, but she didn't bust his balls over it. Annette had a wide mouth and big hair that smelled of coconut oil shampoo. Terry sat talking with her in the kitchen, while the two kids raced in and out of the room. Annette chain smoked Marlboros, wisecracking about Rev. Doben and that pissant DSS worker.

"Fucker didn't know Randy from a hole in the ground!"

Terry couldn't take his eyes off her lipstick, which was the same red-black color as her fingernail polish. She wore faded blue jeans with the knees slashed open and a magenta leotard. Terry could see her nipples pressing against the skintight cloth.

Lorna and Annette had grown up together. They'd partied together, drugged together and dropped out of school together. But when Annette got knocked up she kicked. That was ten years ago, and she hadn't as much as smoked a joint since. She didn't even drink. Sue, her second child, was by the guy she lived with after Jason was born. By then Jason's father was in the big house for armed robbery. Sue's was a fisherman, who went south and stayed there. Just as well, Annette claimed, because when the son of a bitch wasn't beating the piss out of her he was fucking the neighbor's wife, who eventually joined him in Florida. Forget the child support.

Still, Annette made a good home for her kids. Between

welfare and what she earned under the table cleaning houses, their subsidized apartment was spotless. After the confusion at his house, with Lorna either high or strung out because she couldn't afford to score, all of them waiting for Randy to show his face, Terry liked being at Annette's. He liked the way Annette and her girlfriends treated him. One afternoon while they were sitting around the kitchen table Evie teased him.

"Terry, you're gonna break some little girl's heart."

She stroked his biceps.

"Now don't get fresh with my godson," Annettte warned.

"Hey, you guys are family. *I* can do what I want with him!"

"Says who?"

"Says me."

Evie leaned over to brush Terry's cheek with her bright pink lips.

At that Annette got up and put her arms around Terry.

"I just want you to know he's mine."

Slowly she massaged Terry's neck.

"Evie's right," Annette said, pressing her breasts against his back. "You're gonna be a lady killer. How long you been workin' out?"

Terry felt himself blush.

"Coupla years."

"Coupla more years you're gonna do more than break hearts."

That night after the kids were in bed Terry and Annette sat up watching TV. They listened to Leno for a while and then they clicked on HBO for a re-run of "Pretty Woman" with Julia Roberts and Richard Gere. Halfway through the movie Annette stood up.

"Let me make the bed up for you."

She started pulling the couch out. As she bent over the sheet Terry stared at the outline of her highcut leotard under the skintight jeans. Annette was barefoot and her hair fell over her face. She shook her head, flipping the long red finger curls back in place. Terry knew she caught him looking at her ass.

"Okay, beddie bye." Annette patted the bedcovers with the palm of her hand.

As Terry lay in bed he could hear Annette in the bathroom. The pipes banged when she turned the faucets in the sink off. Then Annette flushed the toilet. He heard her footsteps padding down the hallway. A door creaked. After that the house was still. The digital clock on the table said two o'clock. Terry shifted under the covers. He felt tired, but he couldn't manage to drop off to sleep.

He lay there in the dark thinking about Randy, dead two weeks now and under the ground in Beechbrook Cemetery, where the fishermen who weren't Catholic were buried. When Terry was in grade school, the teacher used to take the class there for Memorial Day. They would put flowers on the graves, placing wreaths at the foot of the stones. Then Ms. Garlick would tell them stories from the days of sail, when captains called "highliners" raced each other to bring the swift schooners to port, their holds bursting with cod. Back in class, she showed the kids pictures of dories bobbing on the high seas, as the men hand-lined the big fish even in rain or snow. There was one photograph that Terry never forgot. Taken in 1900 from the top of Banner Hill in East Gloucester, it was a panoramic view of Gloucester harbor, from Rocky Neck out to Ten Pound Island, showing dozens of schooners at their moorings or being unloaded at wharves teeming with activity. Behind them were the sail lofts and machine shops that catered to an industry nobody believed would ever die.

"Just imagine, there were once four hundred sail in Gloucester harbor," Mrs. Garlick told the kids excitedly. "Boys didn't go to college then, they went to sea with their dads."

Terry thought that maybe he would go fishing. In two years, when he turned sixteen, he could quit school and get a site. That is, if any boats were left by then. He wondered what it might feel like lying in a bunk on a dragger, far out on Georges where his grandfather fished. Randy had fished there, too, when he was straight; and Terry remembered when the money was good. His parents lived together then on Taylor Street and Carmen wasn't born yet.

It seemed a long time ago that they made a family. Like most of their neighbors, Randy went to sea and Lorna worked on fish. She would drop Terry off at his grandmother's before heading over to Empire's or O'Donnell-Usen to cut and pack haddock or cod fillets that were frozen and shipped around the world. When she picked him up at night, she smelled of fish. So did his father when he came home. And he smelled of booze because he always stopped in at the Old Timer's Tavern or Mitch's before he got back to the house. In those days, flush from his share,

Randy always brought him a surprise. After Carmen was born she got something too. If Randy rolled in late, too drunk to talk, they'd find the presents alongside of their pillows, a new Corgi car for Terry, and Barbie dolls for Carmen.

Seeing Julia Roberts naked in the bathtub gave him that tingling feeling he experienced sitting close to Annette in front of the TV or when she hugged him that afternoon with Evie. He thought of the way the two women smelled of perfume and shampoo and of the breathy way Annette talked as she blew the cigarette smoke out of the corner of that wide mouth that made it seem like she was always smiling. Then he thought about the last time he and Dina had kissed in her parents' living room. They had been kissing and touching until they heard her mother come in the front door.

Lying on his back in the hide-a-bed Terry heard the muffled sounds of ships' engines from the waterfront. He wanted to sleep, but he felt an excitement running through his body. Reaching down under the covers he began to play with himself. He wanted to keep doing it, but he was afraid of getting the sheet wet.

Just as he was dropping off to sleep he felt a weight next to him on the bed. He could smell Annette's hair as she pulled the covers gently aside. Then he felt the warmth of her naked body against his.

For as long as Terry stayed with her, maybe two or three more weeks, Annette came into his bed each night. Sometimes they talked a little. Mostly it was Annette who whispered to Terry, moaning in his ear as she rocked back and forth on top of him, breathing on his face, the taste of her toothpaste on his lips. He loved the firmness of her body that could be so soft, too, as her breasts rested on his chest and he moved his hands down her back.

But then Lorna got out of the hospital and wanted Terry home with her. DSS said he could go back, but not Carmen. Lorna had agreed to enter the methadone program. She was in day treatment, too, and nights she went to meetings. Seeing his mother straight Terry couldn't believe his eyes. But everybody commented on how skinny Lorna had gotten all of a sudden. She didn't eat—she said she didn't have any appetite.

Finally one morning she couldn't get out of bed. After Terry left for school, she lay there until he came home again. The first thing Terry smelled when he came into her room was shit. Right away he called Annette.

"Omigod," she said when she saw Lorna. "This is one sick puppy."

Again the ambulance came, but this time DSS had other ideas. The worker said Terry had to go to an approved placement. Annette rolled her eyes when the woman's back was turned. On the way out she hugged Terry.

Terry was placed in a new home. Jackie his foster mother was a big woman with a good disposition. She had a couple of kids of her own and a girlfriend named Tina, who slept in her bed with her. They let him come and go as he pleased.

After the news leaked out that Lorna had cancer, the teachers were lenient. Terry liked school, even though his marks didn't always show it. He was good at math and the teachers let him spend a lot of time in the new computer lab. Sometimes he'd stay after school playing games and surfing the Internet until the custodian came in and told him they were locking up.

Terry liked being alone in front of the big color monitor. He looked at the pictures from the Hubbell Space Telescope and wondered what the universe out there was really like. Sitting by himself in the quiet school connected to the Internet, he remembered those nights at Annette's house. He wanted to visit her again, but he felt too shy to show up at the apartment. He tried to recall what Annette's hands felt like as they caressed his back and chest, her lips against his ear as she whispered meaningless phrases.

One night they had joked that what Annette initiated was child molestation.

"I could do time," she whispered. "Would you turn me in?"

When Terry said he wouldn't, that he liked what they did, Annette kissed him softly with her big wet lips until he got hard again. And then she slipped him gently inside her and started rocking again and moaning until he thought he would die.

Thinking about those nights with Annette, Terry typed in "sex" on the search engine. When he got a list of websites he started clicking on the hyperlinks. One said "teenage sluts." Calling it up, he came to a home page called PinkButts that advertised itself as the "teen sex wonderland." When he entered he found a high resolution photograph of a blond girl leaning forward to suck a guy's cock.

Under her lay another girl who was playing with her tits.

Terry couldn't believe what he was seeing. As he continued clicking on the preview buttons he found stacks of thumbnail pictures of naked men and women. Enlarged, one showed a woman on her knees, her face smiling back at the viewer. She had slipped one of her hands under her stomach letting her fingers spread open the lips of her cunt. In the following image she was sitting naked on a guy's face. When Terry clicked the "next" button, information came on about how you could become a member by using your credit card.

The next day in school he told Dina about what he had discovered on the Net. She stayed after with him. When the rest of the kids left the computer room and the teacher was gone, Terry showed Dina the preview pictures from PinkButts. Then they went to another site called Nasty Pussy Online. When Terry clicked on the following page they saw a young blond girl on top of a guy. Her head was turned to the viewer, her eyes closed, mouth open in a moan of ecstasy.

"Omigod, they're actually fucking!" Dina said.

Terry could hear the excitement in her breath.

"How do we get in there?" she asked.

"You gotta pay with a credit card?"

"I could take my mother's."

"She'd find out."

Dina smiled.

"Mrs. Granese," she said. "She leaves her pocket book everywhere."

"Let's just forget it," he told Dina.

"No way! I'm gonna see those gay guys playing with each other."

The next day after school, Dina got into Mrs. Granese's pocketbook and found a Visa card. An hour later she and Terry had subscribed to five different adult sex sites. When Dina's friend Michelle found out, she started staying after school.

"Awesome!" she shouted as she watched a video clip of a guy stroking himself.

Meanwhile Terry and Dina had found a site that showed cheerleaders mooning the crowd. Next thing you knew they were down on the grass eating each other out.

When it got around that Dina and Terry knew how to log onto the X-rated websites, more kids started showing up at the lab after school. The teachers thought it was great they were demonstrating a new interest in this technology. But as soon as Mr. Lannon or Mrs. Granese left the room, everybody started clicking on the thumbnails Terry and Dina had book-marked. Some enterprising kid found a pornographic story site. Pretty soon everybody was reading about a teenage boy who went to visit his young aunt and ended up in bed with her.

There were so many kids interested in learning about computers the lab was crowded during study hall and even after school. An article appeared on the Gloucester Daily Times weekly education page congratulating the ninth grade for entering the digital age so enthusiastically. Then one day Mrs. Granese caught Donny Albuloni with his pants down around his knees. He was jacking off in front of a full-size picture of Princess Di giving head to some guy dressed like a palace guard. Once the faculty started monitoring the computer lab, attendance fell off. Not long after that Mr. Granese got his monthly Visa statement.

At first, the story got out that Mr. Granese, a fisherman who went to bed early and got up before dawn, thought his wife had subscribed because she wasn't getting enough. But when the teachers started checking the computers against Mr. Granese's Visa bill, they found a dozen more sites book-marked, including Ass Alley, for people addicted to spanking and sodomy. That's when the shit hit the fan.

The school installed filters in all the computers. Then the principal tried to isolate the suspected ringleaders. He hauled Terry and Dina into his office, questioning each one separately. Both denied any involvement, as did the rest of the kids. Meanwhile, some young hackers managed to break into the computers at the Sawyer Free Library. When an elderly volunteer, who happened to be passing by them one afternoon, caught sight of a naked woman with two guys ejaculating onto her tits, she screamed, waking up all the homeless men asleep in the lounge chairs. Instantly the other patrons were on their feet. The hackers escaped in the confusion.

The following day the paper ran a story linking the two events, followed by an editorial that called for measures to keep minors from accessing what they called "obscene material on the Net." Demanding complete censorship, members of Families First blamed the scandal on permissive teachers. Civil libertarians responded, claiming that kids had been forced into covert behavior because the schools lacked adequate sex education.

Since the school couldn't punish the entire ninth grade, they brought in therapists from the Mental Health Center to help the kids process what they'd been exposed to. For three days in a row everybody was forced to attend assemblies where they talked about recovering from trauma. Then they broke down into small discussion groups, led by social workers and guidance counselors.

Terry sat listening to one woman ask the girls how it felt to see members of their own sex violated like that.

"Hey, they get paid for it, don't they?" Carla Gadbois shouted out.

When the counselor said it was only natural for them to be in denial, the kids told her that sex was sex and everybody did it. After that they refused to participate. They figured the adults would eventually relent in their desire to get back to academics, finishing the school year within the 180 days mandated by the state.

By then Terry and Dina had a new routine. They stopped at Michelle's house after school every day where the three of them watched videos from her father's porn collection.

At first they all sat on the couch in the basement rumpus room. The girls smoked and Terry would take a can of Rolling Rock out of the refrigerator behind Michelle's father's bar. The TV was big screen so the acts of sex in the movies seemed a lot more realistic than when they saw them on the Internet

"Omigod," Dina said watching some guy's prick get stiff.

Michelle turned to Terry.

"Do you get that big?"
Terry felt his face redden.
"Let us see," Michelle said.
"No way," Terry said, concentrating on the screen.
"If you show us we'll strip for you. Right, Dina?"
"I don't know," Dina said.
"I ain't afraid," Michelle said, lifting up her T-shirt. She stood in front of the screen in her bra and blue jeans
"Come on," said Michelle, unzipping her jeans.
Dina pulled her T-shirt off.
"Now you," Michelle said to Terry.
Watching the girls stripping, Terry felt himself getting aroused. Michelle came over to where he sat.
"Here, let us do it."
She reached down where Terry sat and began to unbutton his plaid shirt.
"I can undress myself, for Crissakes!"
"You're not quick enough," Michelle said, sliding out of her jeans. Terry looked at her belly button buried in the softness of her stomach.
"Help me pull this thing out," Michelle said, grabbing the handle under the couch. Pretty soon she had thrown the cushions on the floor. The Queen-size bed slid out, taking up most of the room in front of the TV. Naked, the three of them lay back on the mattress, Michelle and Dina on either side of Terry.
"It's pretty big," Michelle said, looking over at Terry's cock. "Have you ever seen it, Dina?"
"I ain't tellin'."
"D'you ever take it in your mouth?" Michelle asked,

stretching out.

Terry looked at Michelle's tits, but he didn't want Dina to think that he preferred them to hers. Actually Dina's were nicer even though they weren't as big.

Just then the guy in the film lay back while one girl played with him and he sucked the other's tits. Michelle reached out and the next thing Terry knew she was jerking him off.

At first Terry thought Dina would be mad, but she smiled as she watched Michelle slowly moving her fingers up and down Terry's prick. Then Dina came over and started to kiss Terry.

"Oh wow!" Michelle said, letting her free hand slip between her legs the way one of the girls on the screen was doing it.

With Dina and Michelle naked on each side of him and Michelle's fingers around his prick Terry couldn't hold it any longer. Michelle squealed as he came all over her hand. While the three of them lay still watching the movie, Terry put his arm around Dina and pulled her down next to him. Michelle snuggled on his right side and no one said anything until the movie ended and they had to get up and get dressed before Michelle's parents came home from work.

After that first day the sex got serious. They didn't even need the videos to get turned on. Once in a while only one girl showed up, so Terry got to fuck Dina by himself and he and Michelle had their time too. If the girls found themselves alone they had sex with each other. The next day they told Terry what they did and all three of them got off on it.

When Terry came in the house one night, Jackie told him that Lorna had called looking for him. After supper she drove Terry over to Friend Street, waiting downstairs for him in her big blue and tan Bronco.

At first when Terry saw the frail figure across the room he thought it was some old lady. Then he recognized his mother in the Barcalounger. Lorna seemed to have shrunk in size. Bending over to kiss her Terry caught a smell like that of a dead animal in the wall.

"It's me all right." Lorna's voice wheezed out of her chest.

"Ma, you're so thin."

"The *cansuh*," Lorna whispered. "There's nothin' left of me."

"Where's Carmen?"

"They don't think it's good for her to see me so sick."

Terry sat on the footstool near his mother's chair. Lorna's feet looked gray in her faded green paper slippers.

"Look," she said. "I gotta tell you about some business."

Terry was shocked at Lorna's condition. Why wasn't she in the hospital?

"I'm gettin' your father's life insurance," Lorna said. "It's in your name and Carmen's. He had it from the Seafarer's Union. His pension, too. There's gonna be death benefits from Social Security until you and your sister turn 18."

When Lorna started to cough, Terry thought she was going to throw up. The convulsions made her bend over, her head flopping back and forth like she was drunk or high.

"I just thought you should know," Lorna went on hoarsely. Then she started to cry.

"I ain't been there for you. But at least you'll get something from your father."

"Ma, you tried." It was all Terry could think to say.

"You're okay with Jackie?"

"Yeah, she's great," Terry said.

On the way down the stairs Terry could still smell that rotting smell. It seemed to stick in his nostrils.

The next day at school Michelle told Terry and Dina that her father suspected someone had gotten into his video collection.

"He says I can't bring anybody home," she said.

Lying on his bed at Jackie's after school everyday Terry missed those afternoons with Dina and Michelle. Sometimes he did homework, but mostly he thought about the things all three of them had done together. One night Jackie suggested that he go back to the Y.

So Terry walked over to Middle Street after school. He signed up for the weight room and then he went to use the Nautilus equipment. Before showering he usually took a swim. Working out did make him feel better.

One day Zack, an older guy most of the kids knew, approached Terry.

"Big boy like you could make a little money," he said.

"Yeah, how?" Terry figured Zack had something lined up on the waterfront.

"You like the chickies?"

"Who me?"

Zack told him to come over to his house on Cherry

Street after school the next day.

"Twenty bucks an hour," Zack said.

"For what?"

"You'll see."

When Zack opened the door, Terry saw a couple of high school girls sitting in the living room. They had drinks in their hands and one of them was smoking a joint. They both smiled when Zack led Terry in. Pretty soon Terry had settled down with a can of Rolling Rock. He took a toke as a second joint came around. Then Jack invited them into the studio. It was set up like a bedroom with lights on stands in a circle around the bed.

At first Terry didn't get it, but when he saw the girls beginning to strip he knew what they'd all be paid to do. Zack stood behind a couple of complicated looking cameras. Next to them was a Camcorder.

"Basically there's no scenario," Zack explained. "Hannah and Jen have done this before, but you'll get the hang of it."

Terry watched the two girls who were both naked now. There was a world of difference between their bodies and Dina and Michelle's. They had firm asses and Jen's legs were incredible. As they led him to the bed, Zack started the Camcorder. Then Hannah and Jen began to take Terry's clothes off.

"Enjoy!" Zack shouted as he moved the Camcorder, stopping occasionally to get some still shots.

The girls were good. They got Terry naked and down on the bed with them. With each of them touching him all over Terry had an instant erection.

"No problem with wood here!" Zack yelled out. "Let's roll!"

After the session, Zack paid them all in cash. When Terry got home that night he couldn't believe what he'd done. Still, he had forty bucks in his pocket and he'd had sex with two fantastic girls. Zack had told them not to hold back and the girls didn't. Once Terry got over the presence of the cameras, he did fine. He wondered if this was the way they made the porn videos they watched at Michelle's.

When Dina asked him where he'd been, he told her that he was spending a lot of time with his mother.

"Yeah, right. Sitting up there watching her sleep."

But the sessions with Zack ended abruptly. The cops raided his house one night, carting away prints, negatives and video tapes. The story made the front page of the Gloucester Times. Terry heard Jackie and Tina talking about it after dinner.

"There's a sicko for you," Tina said, "exploiting kids like that."

Terry wondered if they'd be looking for him. The girls had to be at least eighteen but he was under age. The article didn't say anything about the models, that they'd done it willingly or been paid by Zack. There was no mention of the drugs and booze. All it said was that Zack was out on bail and the case was under investigation by the State Police Vice Squad.

Terry was scared shitless when he went to school the next day, but nothing happened. When he got home, Jackie was waiting to tell him the news that his mother had disappeared. After her chemo that morning they'd sent her in the ambulance back to the apartment to recuperate. A visiting nurse was supposed to look in on her. By the time she arrived with the Hospice worker Lorna was gone. No one had seen her go and they had no idea where she might be.

"The doctor says she's weak. God knows how long she'll hold up," Jackie said.

After supper the DSS worker called.

"Oh my fucking Jesus!" Jackie shouted as the two women talked on the phone. When she got off the line, Jackie came over to where Terry was sitting in front of the TV.

"Here's the poop," she said. "Your mother got some humungous check in the mail. She was supposed to put it in a separate account for you kids. Instead, she cashed it. No one knows where she went."

That night in bed Terry wondered why his mother didn't deposit the money as she told him she would. Lorna had her own disability benefits. That check was supposed to be Carmen's and his. But he knew better. You just don't wave a couple of bills like that in front of an old junkie.

Lorna's story didn't make the paper at all. Just as well because Terry didn't want any attention drawn to him. He even stayed away from Dina and Michelle. He went to the Y after school and he came straight home.

When the cops were at the door a week later, Terry figured his luck was over. But they didn't come to arrest him or even to ask him any questions. They came to tell him that his mother was dead. Lorna's charred body had been found in the wreckage of an old house that burned down on Pleasant Street the night before. There was evidence of an enormous amount of drugs.

A couple of days later, a junkie everyone knew as Julius confessed to being in the house with Lorna. There were maybe a dozen druggies crashing in the ramshackle Victorian, he told the cops. When word got around that Lorna had received the check, some of her old shooting friends prevailed upon her to cash it. They scored big time. Then they took her with them to the abandoned house. All of them lay around doing everything they'd ever dreamed of doing— horse, crack, coke, methamphetamines, ludes. Every junky in town eventually showed up for the party. It went on for days. Lorna was in the middle of it all, Julius reported, lying on her mattress like a queen holding court.

One night it got chilly, Julius said. Some idiot tried to start a fire in the fireplace. The flue must have been blocked. The next thing they knew the house was on fire. Flames shot out of every hole in the walls. Everybody split leaving Lorna behind. By the time the fire trucks arrived, it was too late to save her.

Lorna wanted to die, Julius insisted. It was a choice, he said, between the chemicals she liked or the ones they were pumping into her.

"Oh, man, did we get high!" he squealed as the detectives led him away to be booked.

Annette and Evie organized a memorial service for Lorna. A hundred people attended and Terry felt that it was the kind of recognition that his mother deserved. After the funeral the cops came again. They wanted Terry to go with them. At the station they had all of Zack's pictures spread out on a desk top. Terry had never seen any of them. When he looked at himself naked with Hannah and Jen, it seemed like he was watching strangers doing things in some distant, unconnected way.

Terry figured he didn't have anything to lose. He told the detectives everything. He produced the money Zack had paid him, twelve twenty dollar bills. He hadn't even known what to spend it on, he said.

The cops told Terry that if he testified against Zack, admitting that he had been coerced into acts of sex, he'd be out of the doghouse. But Terry figured that he'd done what he'd done because he wanted to, not because he'd been compelled to do it.

"What about the money?" the interrogator asked.

"I would of done it for nothing," Terry said.

Since Zack didn't have sex with Terry or the girls or make any attempt to sell the photographs and tapes, he received a two-year sentence for possession of child pornography, meaning pictures of Terry, and sexual exploitation of a minor. The judge suspended one year of it for first offense. Terry was ordered to undergo a psychiatric evaluation. After interviews with two doctors and a clinical psychologist, he was found to be suffering from post-traumatic stress disorder, due to his parents' deaths. Weekly counseling was mandated.

Since Terry was three years away from emancipation, he stayed with Jackie and Tina, who banked Randy's Social Security death benefits each month for him, hoping that someday Terry might use them to pay for college or trade school. Carmen was put up for adoption. After school let out Terry worked in the Summer Youth Program as a playground supervisor. In September he went to high school with Dina and Michelle, who were both pregnant. Just before Christmas each had her baby. A girl for Michelle and a boy for Dina. By spring the girls were wheeling the babies around town. Terry met them on the Boulevard after school each day. All three of them walked together past the Man at the Wheel, Terry in the middle, Dina and Michelle on either side. Looking down at little Terry in his pram and his half-sister Kristen in hers, Terry had a big smile on his face.

Checks

Everybody knew when the checks came. Growing up in the Park, you learned that Social Security came on the first day of the month. Disability arrived on the third. Welfare checks were issued twice a month, on the first and third or second and fourth weeks, depending on whether the last two digits in your Social Security number were even or odd. Veteran's benefits came monthly; Workmen's Comp once a week. If you were out of work, you picked up your unemployment check every other week at the DET office down by the State Fish Pier. The day depended on the first initial in your last name. For those lucky enough to be working, payday was every Thursday.

In Tommy's house his mother collected welfare for him and his two sisters. Uncle Albert received a VA check. He had been wounded in the Korean War and discharged with a Purple Heart. Nobody knew what kind of wound it was, but Albert spent most of his time in bed. When he got up it was generally to cash his check across the street at Manny's Lounge, where the women took their welfare checks.

Albert was older than Tommy's mother Norma. The neighbors thought he looked old enough to be her father. Tommy always thought it was weird that Norma and Albert slept in the same bed. If he was Tommy's uncle wouldn't he be his mother's brother? But it didn't work out that way. Albert wasn't related to Norma. He wasn't related to anyone in the household, although some neighbors claimed that Tommy was Albert's son by Norma.

"He ain't yah uncle," the kids would taunt Tommy. "He's yah old man!"

But when Tommy asked Norma if Albert was his father, she denied it.

"What are you nuts? An old guy like him!"

Still Albert didn't treat his nieces and nephew like an uncle should. He shouted at them from bed to bring him his effing tea or to get those shit-faced dinner plates out of the way. Lounging in the bedroom in pajamas all day, the TV going full blast, Albert didn't act like anyone's relative. He screamed at the kids, making vicious remarks about the Blacks and Latinos who came into the apartment. Often they were the children of Jamaican truck drivers the women in the Park picked up at Manny's. Some even stayed in the Park with their white girlfriends. After they left a black baby would be born, or one that looked Mexican or Puerto Rican. That really got Albert worked up.

"Niggers and spics, spics and niggers," he'd yell. "Didn't I fight a war to keep them sumbitches outta this country?"

When Tommy or his sisters complained about Albert's behavior, Norma told them to zip it up.

"He's your uncle and he's gonna do and say what he wants."

"But Ma," Tommy said. "None of our friends will come over and play."

"Take them the hell outside!"
"What if it's too cold."
"Tough titty."

Albert's temper wasn't half the problem. Tommy could block his ears or just make believe Albert wasn't there when he got heated up. What Tommy couldn't do was keep Albert's hands off him. It started when Tommy was five. Once, when Norma was out shopping, Albert came into the kitchen where Tommy was playing on the floor with his firetruck. He sat down heavily at the table, sliding a tea mug back and forth across the Formica surface so that it made a scraping sound. When Tommy started to get up his uncle grabbed him. He'd never seen Albert move so fast. The next thing he knew Albert was standing behind him. He pushed Tommy over on the breakfast table and pulled his jeans and his underpants down. Reaching into the margarine dish Albert stuck his fingers into the melted yellow mound and slathered it between Tommy's legs. Tommy felt this hard slippery thing at his behind. Albert grabbed him around the neck with one hand. With the other hand he spread the cheeks of Tommy's ass and shoved that greasy thing in, putting his hand over Tommy's mouth as Tommy screamed in pain.

Up and down Albert pushed into Tommy's asshole until Tommy thought he was going to split in two. He felt Albert's breath on his neck as Albert's body shook with the exertion. Then he felt something wet like an enema shooting up into his guts. Finally Albert pulled that thing out. As he fell back onto the kitchen chair, he pulled Tommy down onto his lap, jeans and underpants dangling around

Tommy's ankles. Tommy could smell Albert's sour breath.

"One word and I'll kill you," he whispered hoarsely into Tommy's ear.

When it happened again Tommy tried to fight Uncle Albert off, but Albert was strong for an invalid. This time Albert got Tommy over his knees on the bed and started spanking him.

"Cry, you little shithead," Albert shouted as he moved Tommy back and forth across his lap. Then Albert gasped and pushed Tommy off his lap. Tommy fell on the floor just as Norma came in with the groceries.

"I had to wail the little fucker's insubordinate arse," Albert said.

"Do it for me, too," Norma said going back into the kitchen.

The third time Albert managed to get Tommy face down onto the bed. Pulling his shorts off he tied his legs to the bottom bedposts and his hands to the headboard. Then he started beating Tommy's legs and thighs with a belt. When Tommy cried out, Albert stuffed Tommy's underpants in his mouth. After that he climbed on top of Tommy and stuck his thing up Tommy's ass. Tommy felt Albert's saliva dripping on his neck as Albert pushed and slobbered all over him. Afterwards he thought he'd never stop shitting.

Once he started school Tommy went wild. He shoved the kids who were ahead of him in the cafeteria line. He beat girls up at recess, he sassed the teachers. After six months of Tommy's behavior the principal called Norma in. Ms. Parks told her that Tommy was making it impossible for anyone to learn in the classroom. She said they would have to have him evaluated under Chapter 766.

Norma didn't know what that meant, but she told the principal to go for it.

"Hey, I can't control him at home."

Tests showed Tommy to be a hyperactive child. The school adjustment counselor said he thought Tommy had Attention Deficit Hyperactive Disorder. He told Norma that the doctor suggested putting Tommy on medication. They wanted to try Ritalin.

"Don't you think he's too young for nerve pills?" Norma asked.

"They aren't exactly that," Mr. Tibbets, the counselor said. "We'd just like to quiet him down."

"So would I!"

The counselor turned to Norma.

"Let me ask you something." His face looked like he'd had too clean a shave that morning. "Is there anything happening at home that might be affecting Tommy?"

"Like what?"

"Some family stress maybe. Or do you suppose anyone is hurting Tommy?"

"No way!"

"The school has heard about a relative who lives with you," Mr. Tibbets went on. "We understand he's the children's uncle."

"What's that got to do with Tommy's behavior?"

"It depends upon his relationship to Tommy, and to you, too."

That night at home Tommy heard Norma talking in

the bedroom with Uncle Albert.

"Tibbets wanted to know if you're really Tommy's uncle. Faggot asked me what *role* you played in the family."

Tommy didn't catch Albert's answer. But his uncle seemed to keep his distance after that. The Ritalin didn't work. In fact, Tommy got more impulsive than usual, smashing his lunch dishes in the cafeteria when the noon supervisor told him to pile them up right, darting from one end of the school bus to the other while the driver tried to concentrate on getting the kids off in one piece.

One day Tommy came home from school just in time to catch Albert with Tommy's little sister Robin on his knee. She was naked from the waist down and Albert was trying to stick his fingers between her legs. Grabbing a knife from the sink Tommy rushed across the room. He slashed at Albert's hands. Albert jumped up letting Robin fall to the floor. Blood dripped from his hands as he chased after Tommy. But Tommy was quick. He slipped around the table.

"Go find Ma next door," he shouted at Robin.

Albert was breathing hard. He couldn't get his hands on Tommy.

"You little fuck!" he shouted, wiping a lacerated hand on his pajama leg.

"What the hell is all this?"

Norma shouted as she came in the door.

"Sumbitch cut me," Albert screamed.

Norma went after Tommy, but he managed to get to the door and out into the corridor. Hearing the commotion, some neighbors came running out of their apartments. When they saw the blood on Albert's hands, they just stood there.

"Mind your own business," Norma shouted. "When we really need you, you ain't there."

That night Albert woke up with chest pains. Tommy could hear him gasping for breath as Norma called the ambulance. On the way to the hospital Albert died. Norma came home sobbing. She went into their bedroom and closed the door. Neighbors looked after Tommy and his two sisters until the funeral.

Norma stood crying while the American Legion buried Albert in his uniform. Tommy watched the coffin being lowered into the ground at Oak Grove. He listened to the chaplain's prayer and to the bugler playing taps. But he didn't feel sad. He didn't feel anything at all.

After Albert's death the house seemed empty. It was just Norma now with Tommy, Robin, and the baby Jessica. Norma had trouble getting up in the morning, so the neighbors helped make breakfast for the kids. They put Tommy and Robin on the school bus. A van from Child Development took Jessica to day care.

Tommy went days without shitting. Either he wouldn't shit or he couldn't, the pediatrician said when Norma finally took him in. When the doctor asked if anything was bothering him, Tommy just shook his head. He refused to take the laxative the doctor prescribed. After two weeks he smelled like shit, it came right out of his pores. The whole house smelled that way, and the two girls started complaining.

On the phone, the doctor told Norma to give Tommy an enema. She went over to Connor's Drug Store and bought a box of Fleets. When she tried to get Tommy to bend over so she could stick the enema in, Tommy went crazy. He hit Norma, knocking the enema on the bathroom floor. Then he ran out of the house. The police had to bring him back. Tommy was swollen with shit, but he wouldn't let it go. Finally, the pediatrician came up with an idea. He found a laxative that could be secretly mixed with Tommy's food. Once Tommy ate it, he began to shit. At first he took such a big shit that the toilet overflowed and they had to call the maintenance crew.

At school they placed Tommy in a Special Ed class. But he wouldn't sit still. He raced around the room, knocking other kids down. He pissed in his pants and sat in it all day. The teachers tried everything, but they couldn't get Tommy to read with the group or even participate in class activities like making animals out of Silly Putty and writing the different names on oak tag labels.

At home after school Tommy couldn't be managed. No sooner was he home than he was out the door. He didn't come back until dark. Even at that, Norma had to go looking for him all the way up Cleveland Street.

One day Tommy was playing with a can of charcoal lighter he found out in the yard near someone's grill. He squirted it at the girls who started running away from him and Stevie Drolette. Then Mrs. Cardoza's cat Dolly appeared. She was what the old ladies called a "money cat" because she had calico markings. Tommy grabbed Dolly around the neck and squirted lighter fluid on her fur. When Dolly started kicking and scratching with the claws on her back legs, Tommy threw her down on the asphalt driveway and held her there with his foot. Stevie ran to get a book of matches from his mother's kitchen. The kids stood aghast as Tommy lit one and touched it to Dolly's fur.

Dolly went up in flames as Tommy removed his foot from her body. She ran in circles while the girls stood screaming. Just then Mr. Jackman from the next entry appeared. When he saw Dolly on fire he tossed his Levi jacket over her body and held her down under it. Then somebody had called the police. The vet had to give Dolly a shot to put her out of her misery. Mrs. Cardoza didn't say anything. Every day after that she stood in the hallway looking in the direction of Norma's apartment. Tommy saw her eyes fixed on him.

Taken to juvenile court, Tommy was ordered to undergo counseling at the Mental Health Center. Norma had to drag him all the way up Maplewood Avenue and across Poplar Street. After they got to the hospital and were sitting with the therapist, Tommy refused to speak. He sat for an hour with his mouth clamped shut. He did this for three weeks until the therapist gave up and sent them both away.

Then Tommy started stealing. First it was candy bars at the Cape Ann Market, then he'd sneak into the neighbors' apartments looking for money in teapots or bureau drawers. Tommy liked the idea of having money in his pocket. One day he walked into an office on Center Street and started talking to the receptionist. Tommy had a way with most people, who usually found him cute. He'd stand there smiling as he talked to them, but his eyes were always on alert for stuff lying around.

In the office he caught sight of the receptionist's brown pocketbook right on top of her desk. After he said so long, he hung around outside looking in the window to see if she'd leave the room. When she did, he slipped inside, opened the pocketbook, and grabbed a bunch of bills out of the woman's wallet.

First he walked up and down Main Street looking for one of the kids to show them what he'd ripped off. When no one from the Park appeared, Tommy went into Radio Shack and bought a couple of transistor radios with earphones. He took them home, and when he ran into Stevie Drolette he handed one to him.

"What's this?" Stevie wanted to know.

"Shit, man, I just bought it!"

"Where'd you get the dough?"

"I ain't tellin'."

"You didn't get it from your old lady?"

"Are you kidding?"

That night the police were at Norma's door. The receptionist had remembered Tommy telling her he lived at the Park. When she went from store to store asking if some kid had been in with fifty bucks to buy anything, the clerk in Radio Shack remembered Tommy.

Norma begged the police to let her make restitution. But after she did Tommy only stole more. When the psychiatrist the court sent him to for an evaluation asked him how he felt about what he was doing, Tommy said that he didn't feel anything. How could he tell the shrink that all he experienced was a rushing in his head, like something pushing him to touch or grab or hit whatever person or thing was in front of him?

"Do you want to hurt people?" the psychiatrist asked.

Tommy looked down as he scuffed his high tops on the rungs of the chair.

"People want to hurt me."

But when the counselor in school prodded Tommy to find out what he thought, Tommy just shook his head.

"I don't feeling nothin'," he told Mr. Tibbets.

"Don't you think about your mother or your sisters?"

Tommy shook his head again. He didn't know how to tell Mr. Tibbets that it was all a blank inside him. He heard people's voices like they came from far away, he saw them in a fog.

It turned out Tommy could barely read, and he couldn't write his own name. Sometimes it came out "Tomy." Other times he wrote it with a small "t." The Special Ed coordinator tested him again and again. Nothing stayed in his memory. He knew the words for everything and he could talk, even though he didn't say much. It seemed like the only way he could express himself was by kicking the kid next to him or taking things away from people.

The teachers told Norma that Tommy wasn't retarded, but that he appeared to have something wrong with him. None of the tests had revealed brain damage. Maybe he was semi-autistic, they said; or it could be he had some kind of schizoaffective disorder.

"He was fine when he was little," Norma said. "He

talked a lot. Actually he was a pretty sweet kid."

Tommy heard words which meant nothing to him. Looking at Norma and Mr. Tibbets sitting there was like watching TV. Things sort of went on in front of him. Sometimes he listened, but mostly he tuned it all out.

They gave him medications to help him sleep at night and pills to make him behave in school. Now he just sat there while the kids around him made noises. He wished that everything would go black, but he didn't know how to make it happen.

Then he started drinking. At first he and Stevie Drolette stole beer out of their mothers' refrigerators. They drank it in the swamp across the street behind McDonald's. They met some older kids there who told them about parties they went to at night up the tracks. One night Tommy and Stevie sneaked up behind Linsky's junk yard and followed the train tracks into the woods on the way to the reservoir. In a clearing they saw a fire and some guys sitting around it. They watched the men from behind the trees, listening to them talk.

Stevie and Tommy didn't know who the men were, but they soon found out. Some were homeless and they lived in tents or a lean-to up near the reservoir. Others came there to drink at night. Usually the cops left them alone because hidden in the woods the men didn't cause any trouble. They drank, they shot the shit, and sometimes they smoked dope. The younger guys did the dope, the old timers stuck to the booze.

Pretty soon both boys came in by the fire to listen to the older men. Beers got passed around, along with smokes. Tommy didn't like the taste of cigarettes, but dope made him feel good once he got used to inhaling its sharp fumes.

Some of the old timers had been coming there to drink for years. One of them was called Powder. He had a red face and red blond hair. He spent the winter months in a room over Schooner's on Hancock Street, but in the summer he and a couple of the regulars moved out of the rooms to save money. They lived in the woods, using their retirement or disability checks to buy liquor.

Powder had worked for years for the DPW. He got the name Powder because anytime the foreman went looking for him to go out on a job Powder was nowhere to be found. He'd be hiding somewhere in the Public Works barn on Poplar Street, or he'd have crept behind some bushes at a worksite and gone to sleep.

"Taking a powder," the other workers answered when the foreman asked for him. So the name stuck.

Now Powder was out on permanent disability. He drank from when he woke up until he passed out at night. Usually he went to sleep wherever he found himself.

When Powder's SSDI check came to a post office box on the third of the month, he had one of the older kids pick it up for him. They'd bring it back for Powder to sign and then they'd cash it for him at Manny's or in Store 24 on Maplewood Avenue. Powder would give them a six-pack for their trouble, and then everyone would drink.

Once Tommy started drinking and smoking dope, he stayed up the tracks as late as he could, especially on weekends. It was summer vacation. Norma tried to get him to sign up for Summer Youth Corps. She figured she could keep track of him that way, at least during the day. But not even the inducement of a regular paycheck interested Tommy. Once he started hanging out up the tracks, he didn't want to stop. Sometimes he ran errands for the men, picking up cigarettes or a sub at Store 24, a Megabucks ticket at Uncle Moe's. For that they paid him in cash or in beer. Tommy didn't care. If he needed money he knew where to steal it. He knew where everybody in the Park kept their cash.

Tommy did errands for Powder, too; but there was something about Powder that made Tommy nervous. Staring at Powder's blood shot eyes, at his red blond hair that was never cut and his ragged clothes, made Tommy's flesh creep.

Powder didn't know Tommy from a hole in the ground. They never spoke. Nobody spoke person-to-person. The men just bantered across the space of the clearing that had been burned out of the woods by years of camp fires. They yelled insults at each other, they argued. But mostly they drank. They drank and they passed out and then they came to and started drinking all over again.

Stevie told Tommy that he had this idea.

"Did you see all that money Powder gets every month?"

"So what?"

"How's about we steal it?"

Tommy hesitated. He had never stolen money off a person. Usually it was from a pocketbook or a wallet when the owner wasn't around.

"Wait till he passes out and then we'll just lift it."
"What about the other guys?"
"We'll do it when they're not around."
"Powder's never alone."
"Just wait and see."

It was the fourth day of the month and Powder must have gotten his check. Tommy and Stevie knew from the kids who cashed it that Powder received over $700 a month in disability payments. It was too early in the month for him to have spent it all. That night, probably, he'd be asking somebody to buy the booze.

When they got to the tracks, they noticed it was quiet. Powder wasn't around, but Stevie said he knew where Powder hung out. Stevie led Tommy deeper into the woods where they saw an old canvas tent. In front of it a campfire was still smoldering.

"He sleeps here," Stevie said, pulling the tent flap open.

Power was inside on the ground, wrapped in a filthy blanket. The tent smelled of beer and piss and of Powder's feet. His boots lay on the ground, one on its side. The heels of his feet, all crusty with calluses and dirt, stuck out of holes in his socks.

"Here's his pants," Stevie said, lunging for the dirty green workpants Powder always wore.

"Shit, the pockets are empty!"

Just then Powder's eyes flicked open.

"What the fuck?"

"It's just us," Stevie said.

Powder groaned, his head falling back on the ground.

"Maybe he's got it on him," Tommy said.

"Chances are he hid it."

Stevie began slipping the blanket off Powder.

"Jesus," Powder mumbled.

Powder was naked under the blanket and Stevie started hauling on his feet.

"Grab him," he said to Tommy.

Together they pulled Powder out of the tent. As he lay there his pink flesh made something start up in Tommy and Tommy kicked Powder in the side of the head. When Powder's mouth fell open he kicked him again.

"What the hell you doin'?" Stevie shouted. "Help me look in the tent."

Stevie pulled the blanket out and started digging around in the dark tent.

"Fuckshit!" he shouted.

Stevie came back to where Powder was lying. He started to shake Powder by the shoulders.

"Where'd you put it, you asshole?"

Powder lunged at Stevie's hand with his teeth.

Tommy watched Stevie spring back from the naked form on the ground. Then Stevie kicked Powder in the balls. Powder's eyes opened and he started to shout. As Tommy looked at Powder's blood shot eyes, that same feeling came over him again and he went up to Powder and kicked him once more in the head. Then Stevie came up with a boulder.

"Where?" he shouted, holding the boulder over Powder's head.

Just as Powder spit something out of his mouth, Stevie slammed the boulder down on Powder's head. The sound made Tommy's stomach churn. And then Powder started screaming. He tried to get up and crawl away from the boys, but Stevie kicked his balls again and Powder fell on his face, groaning in the dirt near the fire. Just then Tommy saw what looked like a piece of broomstick holding up the tent flap. When he yanked it out of the ground, the front of the tent collapsed. Slowly, as if he was looking at himself from outside, Tommy moved to the fire. He stirred the coals up with the stick, holding the stick there until it caught fire. Then he took it over to where Powder lay on his stomach. Touching it to Powder's balls, he held it there. Powder jerked and moaned, yanking himself around so that he looked directly into Tommy's face.

When Tommy saw the look of hatred in his eyes, when he saw the long hair around Powder's ears, the wet lips, the hands down between Powder's legs as Powder bucked and shook on the ground, cowering before Tommy and Stevie, a sensation that this had happened before flashed through his head. He rushed forward and kicked Powder back down on the ground. He pushed him over on his face and started hitting Powder with the burnt round end of the broomstick. He hit Powder on the side of the head, he hit his back and legs. And then he caught sight of Powder's ass, the thin shanks with dirt on them. He took the broomstick and rammed it in above Powder's burnt balls. At first the stick went nowhere. Pushing harder, Tommy felt something give. Then he concentrated the weight of his entire body behind the stick.

Powder shrieked, his cries echoing around them in the woods. Just then, Stevie rushed forward. Picking up the boulder, he hit Powder on the back of the head. Blood splashed up on Stevie's hands. When he saw the blood, Tommy gave one more push on the broomstick.

Then the boys ran. They ran away from the clearing where the men would be. They headed for the train tracks and they followed the tracks back to Linsky's. In the streetlights Tommy saw the blood all over Stevie. Looking down he saw blood on his hands and he smelled the smell of burning wood. There was blood on his sneakers, too.

"Quick," Stevie said, "It's check night. My mother'll be at Manny's."

But Stevie's mother came in from next door and found them both at the kitchen sink. She shouted for Norma. The two mothers stood there watching Stevie and Tommy, stripped down to their underwear, trying to wash Powder's blood off their hands and their faces.

After arraignment the following morning, the boys were separated. The DA wanted Stevie, who was fifteen, tried for murder as an adult. Tommy was sent to the Juvenile Detention Center awaiting the psychiatric evaluation his Public Defender had asked for. On his first night two kids jumped him in the shower. One held Tommy while the other sodomized him. And when he was done he made Tommy suck the other guy's cock. Two or three or four more came and fucked Tommy repeatedly up the ass. Looking in the mirror he saw himself, jism and blood running down his legs. He saw his face in the steamy glass, the welts where he had been hit and hit again, until he'd fallen on his knees, where the guards found him unconscious.

◇

Kelly and Marie

Kelly was so skinny that nobody could tell she was pregnant. She didn't even know she'd been knocked up until just before the baby came. Kelly couldn't remember how it happened, unless it was that time she was stoned at Trina Longo's party. Donny Ciluffo had tried to get her into Trina's sister Suzy's bedroom. But when they opened the door Suzy was in there giving her boyfriend Jason a blow job. So Donny dragged her into Suzy's parents' bedroom. They put the HDTV on and the next thing Kelly knew she was asleep. When she woke up she couldn't find her jeans. Her panties were on the floor beside the bed and Donny had disappeared.

Still, she hadn't felt anything. If you fucked didn't you know it? When she got up she was wet down there. After she sat on the toilet she felt something slimy running out of her. But she was so high she just thought she was having a period.

She went through most of the winter in school without knowing she had a baby inside of her. She didn't get sick in the morning like some of her girlfriends did. Once the baby started kicking, she got scared and went to the school nurse, who drove Kelly to the hospital. After examining her, the obstetrician said that Kelly had better tell her parents she was going to have a baby. That night, when Kelly tried to talk to her mother, Leanne went ballistic.

She called Kelly a no good slut, and she started slapping her around the kitchen. By the time her father got home, Kelly was packing a bag. She didn't even have time to finish once Earl charged into her bedroom. Grabbing her by the straps on her overalls, he dragged her to the front door, kicked it open, and threw Kelly out into the street.

That was two years ago and she hadn't seen her parents since.

She'd stayed in a shelter, and in transitional housing for teen-age mothers and their babies. At the group home in Danvers two nuns taught life skills classes. They told the girls they had to empower themselves otherwise men would dominate them for the rest of their lives.

"Yeah, right," the girls said behind their backs. They knew that Sister Rosina and Sister Beata Immaculata slept together in a big bed. Sometimes at night they could hear one of them spanking the other.

They held classes in self-esteem, too. Sister Rosina would flash these big orange and green iridescent cards that had sayings on them like, "If you always stay where you've always been, you'll never get where you want to go," and "Tomorrow begins today."

One day in class Sissy Campbell turned to Kelly.

"What do they think, we're retarded or something?"

Kelly had been skinny all her life. When she was growing up everybody said she looked more like a boy than a girl. Her mother didn't help it any by keeping her hair cut short. She had practically no tits, and her waist was the same size as her hips.

As for dates, no boy had ever asked her out. Kelly wasn't ugly—she had a pretty face with big green eyes. Mostly she hung out with a group of girls she'd known since grade school. They met after school at each other's houses. Sometimes they had pajama parties where they talked all night about who was dating who.

Sex sucked, they decided. Guys usually got what they wanted while girls ended up feeling used. Or they got knocked up, like Kelly.

Only Marie said she liked sex. Her and her boyfriend Doug had been doing it for a year. But after he went off to college Marie never heard from him again.

"True love, right?" the girls teased Marie.

Once Kelly was out of transitional housing and living in her own subsidized apartment she felt better. She and Petey got $525 a month from Welfare, along with food stamps and Medicaid. The furniture came from the Salvation Army, but it was better than what they'd had in the shelter. Her AFDC worker Tony even found her a used TV. It was an old black and white Motorola, but Kelly didn't mind because she never watched TV that much.

Petey went to day care while Kelly studied for her GED at the Adult Learning Center in the library. The supermarket was an easy walk from where they lived on Elm Street. Kelly liked taking Petey out. Ladies from the elderly housing across from the market made a lot of him as he sat smiling in a shopping cart,

One night the phone rang. When Kelly answered it

some guy was on the other end telling her he had the hots for her hard little body.

Kelly slammed the phone down, but an hour later it rang again.

"I know you're naked in the bathroom."

Kelly was shaking. First she ran into Petey's room to see if he was all right. Then she checked all the window shades to make sure no one could look in. When she thought about what the guy had said, she knew he must be making it up because the bathroom didn't have a window.

All that night Kelly couldn't sleep. The phone didn't ring again, but she never even closed her eyes.

Next morning, after the day care van came for Petey, Kelly rushed to get ready for class. As she was going out the door the phone rang. Automatically, she answered it.

"Nice tights."

Kelly looked down at the black leggings she always thought made her legs look like two sticks. Quickly she went into the bedroom and pulled them off. Once she had her jeans on, she felt safer.

That night there was only a call from Marie, who Kelly hadn't seen in months. She wanted to come over, but Kelly told her she was tired and was going to bed.

"Maybe tomorrow," Marie said.

"Sure," Kelly answered.

As soon as she put the phone down, it rang again. Kelly was afraid to answer but she did, thinking it might be Marie again.

"Took those tights off."

"Why don't you leave me alone!" Kelly shouted, banging the phone down.

When it rang again she didn't answer. She didn't sleep again that night. The next day was Saturday and there was no GED class. To get away from the telephone she took Petey over to the Boulevard where she pushed his stroller up and down until she was so tired she had to sit on one of the wooden benches.

All around her were the same kids who hung out on nights and weekends. Some of them she knew from school, others were younger. But no one spoke to her. It was like they didn't recognize her with Petey. Kelly sat near the Man at the Wheel looking out to sea. Beyond the Breakwater she could make out the skyline of Boston. She remembered going in on the train once to hear a KISS 108 concert at the Boston Garden, but that was at night and she and her friends had taken the next train home. She never did get to see what the city looked like in broad daylight.

She was eighteen years old and she hadn't even been to Disney World. Her parents never took her anywhere, and they didn't go anywhere themselves. Earl and Leanne worked all day. When they came home at night they fought. All Kelly could remember was them shouting at each other. And when they weren't shouting at each other they got on her case. If she had a dollar for every time Leanne called her a useless slut she wouldn't be on welfare now.

Kelly looked down at Petey asleep in his stroller. It was good she never shouted at him. And she'd never laid a hand on him either, the way her parents did with her. Just as well they didn't have any more kids, even though Kelly had felt lonely growing up without a brother or sister.

She watched the gulls lined up nervously on the railing in front of her. They sat waiting for a piece of bait one of the old guys who were fishing would occasionally toss their way. She looked out across the harbor at Ten Pound Island. It seemed to be rising straight out of the water. All around her she listened to the kids talking and laughing. She heard the sounds of car engines revving, the whine of passing motorcycles. For a minute she forgot the telephone calls, but when Petey woke up she knew she had to take him home for dinner.

All through their meal of Campbell's cream of tomato soup and grilled cheese sandwiches she expected the phone to ring, but it didn't. Only that night, after Petey was asleep, did it ring again. She knew it was stupid to answer, but she did.

"What about your panties?"

Just as she hung up, she heard Marie at the door.

Marie had put on a lot of weight since Kelly had last seen her. Her hair was coal black and she was wearing it in bangs now, cut sharply across her forehead. In the shadows of the hallway Kelly thought she looked Japanese.

"Scarecrow," she said. "Have you quit eating altogether?"

"You know me. I can eat all day and it don't go nowhere."

"Well, don't vanish," Marie said. "Where's Petey?"

First they went into the kitchen where Marie took a six-pack of Rolling Rock out of a paper bag and put it in the fridge. Then Kelly opened Petey's door so Marie could see him.

"What a little angel," Marie said, coming out of the darkened room.

They sat on the living room sofa eating popcorn and drinking beer out of the can.

Kelly hadn't meant to tell Marie about the calls, but Marie noticed how distracted she was.

"What's going on," she asked Kelly. "You in any kind of trouble?"

Kelly told Marie everything and when the phone rang Marie grabbed the receiver.

"Quit calling here, you fucking asshole!" she shouted.

After that the phone didn't ring again and Kelly felt better. Maybe Marie had scared the guy off.

Kicking her Tivas off, Marie leaned back on the couch. She was wearing faded jeans that gripped her heavy thighs. Kelly could see her nipples pressing out from the Grateful Dead T-shirt.

After graduating Marie had gone to work in the industrial park, at a place where they did silk screening. The pay was good and she got a lot of overtime. Enough to buy a new Geo and get her own apartment. But when the company was absorbed in a leveraged buyout, they laid off 450 workers. Marie lost her job. For the past four months she'd been living on unemployment.

"I can't make the rent and keep up the car payments," she complained.

"You could always move back home," Kelly said.

"And let those turds tell me what to do?"

"It was only a suggestion."

"I know you meant well," Marie said, putting her hand on Kelly's arm. "What's up with Earl and Leanne?"

"How would I know?"

"You mean they don't even try to see their only grandchild?"

"Hey, Petey and me could be dead for all they care."

"Parents," Marie said. "Who needs them."

The phone didn't ring all the next day. But Kelly wasn't paying much attention to it. While she gave Petey his bath and fixed dinner for them, she was thinking about Marie's visit. Marie said she'd come back soon and Kelly was looking forward to it. After talking with Marie, really talking about their parents and about that dickhead who was harassing her, she realized that she didn't have any other friends. Ever since she'd left the group home she and Petey had been alone, with only the TV for company. She liked her GED classes and it felt good to be getting ready for the exams. Marie had already finished high school. She told Kelly it was important to have your diploma.

"At least they can't take that away from you," she said.

But Kelly wondered what she'd do even if she finally got her certificate.

"You'll get a good job and you won't have to rely on welfare," one of the volunteers at the center told her.

Mrs. Krandall was a nice person who meant well. She helped Kelly with her math. But Kelly knew that Mrs. Krandall went home at night to a big house in Annisquam. Her husband commuted to work in Boston. During break she'd hear the tutors complaining about how much it cost to send their kids to boarding school. They all seemed to have blond hair styled the same way. And when they spoke it sounded like a code. Kelly knew that no matter how long she stayed in school she would never be the same as they were.

She shared that with Marie the next time she came over.

"It's like Doug and me," Marie said. "In school he was always telling me he loved me. He even asked me to marry him. When I told my parents, my father said, 'Don't you think it's odd he's never invited you home to meet his folks? As soon as that kid goes to college you're history.'"

"At least your parents gave you advice," Kelly said.

"You call that advice, always putting me down?"

"Your father was right, wasn't he?"

"Yeah, right. But when Doug blew me off they only laughed at me, as if it was my own fault."

"You must of felt terrible," Kelly said.

"I felt like shit," said Marie.

That was the way they talked, Kelly and Marie. And when Marie wasn't around Kelly would think about what they said to each other. She liked the deep sound of Marie's voice and she liked the feeling she got when Marie would explain something to her. It felt like those times in school, when she was much younger, and the teacher seemed to be talking just to her. As she listened she imagined herself purring like a cat. But all that stopped when the phone rang and it was that same guy's voice, asking if she liked to play with herself.

"Got mine right here in my hand."

Kelly felt like telling him to jerk himself to death, but the coldness of his voice frightened her. She imagined him being able somehow to see through the walls of the house and into her life. Every time she went to the toilet she had this feeling that he was spying on her.

When she told Marie the next day, Marie said they had to take some action.

"The telephone company can find out where that asshole's calling from," she said. "The same thing happened to a friend of mine. Next thing you know they're arresting this pervert."

Kelly let Marie call New England Telephone, and just to be on the safe side they called the police, too. Next thing they knew a detective was at the door.

"I understand you got a problem caller," he said, as Kelly let him in.

She let Marie explain because she was shaking too much. Every time she saw a cop she'd feel like she'd done something wrong even though she knew she hadn't.

Lieutenant Lombriglia was a fatherly type. He had bright brown eyes and his hair was streaked with gray. Listening to him talk made you feel safer.

"You two women live here together?"

"She's my friend," Kelly managed to say. "Just my son and me's here."

"Do you get scared when this guy calls?"

"It makes me shake," Kelly said.

"That's probably what he wants you to feel," the lieutenant said. "Voice not familiar?"

Kelly shook her head. Marie helped Kelly tell him what

the caller said as the lieutenant wrote it all down.

"The phone tap should help us find where he's calling from," he said. "Once we've located him we'll place him under surveillance. We can even record the calls. As soon as we've done that, you can file a complaint and we'll pick him up."

After that Kelly felt better. And Marie came by a lot more. Sometimes they'd drive up to the Mall in Marie's Geo. Marie even bought a little car seat for Petey, who loved to sit in the back looking out the window at the cars whizzing past them on the highway.

Kelly didn't buy much at the Mall. She couldn't afford to. But it was fun to walk up and down under the big glass dome looking in the shop windows. It was even more fun watching all the other shoppers. Kelly had never seen so many well dressed women. Mixed in with them were kids wearing bellbottoms so wide they swept the floor. And the hair! Nothing like she was used to in Gloucester. These kids had dyed theirs green and purple and it was all greased up in points. One girl's head looked like the Statue of Liberty with spikes sticking out all over it.

Kelly looked forward to the trips with Marie. Petey loved them, too. In the Mall he was all eyes, watching the other toddlers as their mothers wheeled them past, looking in the store windows, pointing at the toys, laughing at the clowns that seemed to appear out of nowhere. Being at the Mall, Kelly thought, was like being on TV. Only it seemed like everyone was looking at you while you looked at them.

One night after they got home from the Mall the

phone rang. Marie had just dropped Kelly and Petey off. Rushing to get Petey to bed, Kelly picked up the receiver without thinking.

"Called the cops. You're gonna pay big time for that one."

Long after the guy clicked off Kelly stood shivering with the phone still in her hand. All she could think of was someone trying to harm Petey. She wanted to call the lieutenant, but she was afraid the guy on the phone would see him coming to the apartment. Maybe she could take Petey and run down to the station. What if the guy was waiting for her outside? What if he figured she might do that?

Instead she called Marie who had just gotten in herself.

"Don't move," she said.

Marie was at her door in about three minutes. Together they put Petey to bed. Then they sat on the couch. Marie had her arm around Kelly. The only light in the apartment was from the lamp on the end table.

"I'm afraid to stay here alone," Kelly said.

"Don't worry," said Marie. "I'm not going anywhere."

That night Marie slept on the couch. The phone didn't ring at all and the next day Marie called Lt. Lombriglia, who said for them to stay on the line for as long as they could when the guy called and then punch *69 as soon as they got off.

There were no calls in the following days, but Marie continued to keep Kelly company. They ate together and they took Petey out together. Just waiting for another call drove Kelly nuts. She had dreams about people trying to break her windows. She woke up in the middle of the night in a cold sweat. Marie heard her screaming one night and rushed into the bedroom.

"I can't take it any more!" Kelly sobbed as Marie hugged her.

"I'm right here," Marie said. "Don't be afraid."

Marie held Kelly. She lay next to her on the bed and held her tight. After a while Kelly felt better. Having Marie there with her was a relief. Her warm body made Kelly feel cared for. Nobody had ever held Kelly and it was a new sensation. Pretty soon she fell asleep in Marie's arms.

In the morning Kelly woke up first. She woke up even before Petey. The first thing she felt was Marie lying next to her, her nightshirt up around her thighs. Kelly just lay there looking at Marie as she slept. She looked at Marie's black hair with the sharp bangs, at her sleeping face which seemed very beautiful.

She remembered Marie before she had put on weight. She remembered how the boys used to whistle at Marie when she walked down the corridor to class in a white Spandex miniskirt. She recalled how even the girls remarked on Marie's full breasts. Kelly could see them now as Marie's nightshirt tightened about her. All this gave her a feeling she'd never had before. It was a tingling feeling on her skin, a rippling in her stomach.

When Petey called out, it was Marie who jumped up.

"I'll get him," she said sleepily.

And Kelly let Marie do it. She lay in bed enjoying the fact that Marie wanted to care for Petey. She wondered if that's what people did when they were married, what one person felt while the other got up to get the baby or start breakfast. Thinking of that Kelly drifted off to sleep. When she woke up, she smelled breakfast cooking. She smelled coffee and eggs. Marie was dressed and in the kitchen. She had Petey dressed too, and he was eating happily in his high chair.

When Kelly came into the kitchen, Marie gave her a hug and Kelly thought for a minute she'd faint right there she was so happy.

That night without even discussing it they slept together in Kelly's double bed. It seemed the natural thing to do. Anyway, the minute it got close to bedtime Kelly started to get frightened again, as if the phone would ring and the guy would be on the line.

Marie put her big arms around Kelly and Kelly fell asleep letting Marie hold her. She could hear Marie breathing next to her, feel her heart beating. She loved the smell of Marie's skin, a mixture of perfumed soap and the warmth of her body.

When the phone finally rang again, the guy's voice sounded far away, but Kelly knew it was the same voice.

"Who's your friend with the big tits?"

"Wouldn't you like to know," Kelly answered, hoping to keep him on the line. But the minute she spoke he clicked off.

That night Marie rubbed Kelly's back and Kelly went to sleep with her head between Marie's breasts. At breakfast Marie spooned Petey's cereal up for him. Kelly sat watching Marie as if she had always been with her.

"Why don't you move in," she said to Marie. "That way you can keep up your car payments."

"It crossed my mind. But won't you lose your subsidy?"

"Hey, I can put you on the lease. What if I was getting married?"

Once Kelly had said that word a strange, warm feeling came over her.

"I could bring a few pieces of furniture," Marie said. "My bed's queen size. That is, if we keep sleeping together."

"I like it." Kelly answered without a thought.

Marie reached over and hugged Kelly.

"Me, too."

That morning Marie gave her notice. The only thing she'd lose by moving out right away was her security deposit. She rented a U-Haul and the two girls dragged her mattress and box spring down the two flights of Marie's studio apartment. They took a couple of chairs and Marie packed most of her clothes. All that was left was some kitchen things, which Marie loaded into cartons they picked up at the Liquor Locker. They put Kelly's bed in the basement with Marie's spare furniture. By supper time Marie was all moved in.

Marie picked up the phone and dialed Valentino's.

"Let's celebrate," she shouted, ordering a large pizza with everything on it.

By the time the delivery boy brought the pizza, Marie had set the table. She lit two candles and filled their glasses with beer.

"No cans tonight," she smiled.

The girls touched glasses as Petey looked on laughing. When Kelly fed him the pizza, he couldn't get enough of the pepperoni.

After Petey was in bed Kelly and Marie turned on Marie's big new Quasar color TV. They sat close together on the couch. Marie said she'd split the rent now with Kelly. With her unemployment check she could manage it, along with her car payment. She said she'd pay for her own food, too, and her share of the utilities.

"I gotta get back to work," she said.

They watched the news about the shutting down of the fishing grounds. It showed a bunch of fishermen picketing the offices of the National Marine Fisheries.

"Why don't they kill us and get it over with?" Benny Lobrano, one of the protesters, was telling the Channel 5 interviewer. "If I can't fish I can't live!"

Then Angelica Santucci came on. She was the president of the Gloucester Fishermen's Wives Association that had organized the demonstration.

"We feed the world," she said. "And now the world turns its back on us."

"She's about four feet tall," Marie said, "but those government regulators who are keeping the boats from fishing are scared shitless of her."

"What's gonna happen?" Kelly asked.

"I don't know," Marie said, "but I won't be getting any job working on fish."

Kelly sat watching, happier than she'd felt for a long time. Petey was sound asleep and here they were, herself and Marie, just as if they had always been together.

In bed that night Marie rubbed her back and she massaged Marie's. Just before she went to sleep Kelly put her face up to Marie's and kissed her on the lips. She had never kissed anyone but Petey and she hadn't even thought about doing it. She just found herself kissing Marie softly on the lips and when Marie hugged her close she drifted off to sleep in the warmth of Marie's big body.

Their days together made a pattern. During the week Kelly went to class and Marie went out looking for work. They shopped together, cooked together, and once Petey was in bed, they sat together on the couch talking or watching TV. Sometimes they'd play cards, or Marie would read magazines while Kelly studied.

In bed they kissed and touched each other until they fell asleep. They ran their hands over each other's bodies. Kelly couldn't wait for bed each night. She loved it when Marie kissed her. And Marie let Kelly suck her breasts. Sometimes Kelly drifted off to sleep with a nipple in her mouth.

One night Marie took Kelly's hand gently. She pressed Kelly's finger down between her legs. Marie spread her thighs and Kelly felt the wetness in her vagina. Slowly Marie moved Kelly's finger around inside her. She slid it up and down all the while kissing Kelly. When Kelly felt Marie's tongue in her mouth she let out a gasp.

"Are you okay?" Marie said softly.

"Everything feels so good."

"That's the way it's supposed to be," Marie said.

Marie showed Kelly just where to touch her and how to move her finger up and down and around in circles. As Kelly followed Marie's urging she heard Marie breathing harder.

"Don't stop!" Marie said.

And Kelly didn't. She kept on moving her finger until Marie arched her back. Then she let her breath out hard.

"Oh," Marie cried. "Oh, my God!"

Then she hugged Kelly. Kelly felt Marie's tears on her cheeks.

"Did I hurt you?"

Marie took Kelly's face in both hands.

"No," she said. "It was perfect."

The next night Kelly let Marie do it to her. All day she thought about it, and when they got into bed together naked Kelly realized she was all wet like Marie had been.

Slowly Marie did the same thing to Kelly. She kissed her deeply and let her fingers slip in and out of Kelly's vagina.

"This little knob," Marie said, letting her finger stop where it felt so good, "this is where the nice feeling comes from."

"You mean that's the clitoris?"

"Right," Marie said. "And just like you touched mine I'm going to play with yours."

Marie's words made Kelly more excited. She lay back and let Marie do everything until she felt like she had to pee.

"Just let it happen," Marie said. "When the feeling starts to build go with it. Put everything else out of your mind."

Marie's deep voice made Kelly even more excited. And Marie's finger felt fantastic.

"Suck my breast," Marie said. "Take my nipple in your mouth."

No sooner had Marie used that word then Kelly started

to breathe harder. She felt her stomach tensing up. Then everything let go and she started bouncing up and down. She couldn't stop.

"Oh!" she cried out.

And just as she cried out she felt Marie rocking her slowly back and forth, back and forth, as the ripples built and her whole body strained into them. Then she let her head fall back on the pillow.

"I came," she said to Marie. "Is that what I just did?"

Marie kept on holding Kelly. She kissed her neck and her face.

"Yes, you did," Marie said.

In the morning after Petey had left, Kelly went from the apartment door back to the bedroom where Marie lay naked under the sheet. She had to be at class in fifteen minutes, but she didn't want to leave Marie's side. She sat on the bed.

"Does this mean we're like those two nuns I told you about in the group home?"

Marie sat up, and the minute Kelly saw her big, naked body, her hair across her mouth, she wanted to take her own clothes off and get back into bed with Marie.

"I think it means we care about each other," Marie said.

"That we're more than just friends?"

"That's how I feel," Marie said.

"I feel—" Kelly hesitated. "I feel like I love you."

When the phone rang that night Kelly picked it up right away.

"I got it," the guy said. "I finally got it. You're a couple of lezzies."

Immediately Marie grabbed the phone out of Kelly's hand.

"Hi, good looking," she said. "What's cooking?"

Kelly could hear the guy's voice.

"Oh, you wanna know what we do," Marie said.

Marie had the phone in one hand. With the other she gave Kelly a thumb's up.

"We're into black tights," Marie said. "Sometimes we wear them to bed at night. Does that turn you on?"

On and on Marie went with the guy.

"Whaddayah think we go braless?"

Kelly continued to hear his excited voice over the line.

"Colors? Hang on and I'll tell you."

Kelly heard the guy shout something. Then the line went dead.

Marie slammed the receiver down. Then she picked it up again and punched *69.

"I got him," she shouted. "I think I trapped the son of a bitch. He knew it, too. He was ripshit when he realized I'd kept him talking."

The next morning Lt. Lombriglia called. He asked the two women to stop by and swear out a complaint. As they entered the District Court building Kelly was afraid. What would the cops ask them? Would they find out that she and Marie slept together?

Lt. Lombriglia was patient with them both. He had the papers ready for Kelly to sign. Turns out the guy lived on the next street over. He was in his forties and single, with a record of harassing women over the telephone.

"Once we bring him in and book him," the Lieutenant

said, "we'll tell you. If I know the judge he'll be walking the streets again. But we'll keep a watch on him until the hearing."

"What if he starts calling again?" Marie said.

"Just notify us and we'll pick him right up."

That night in bed Kelly told Marie that she wouldn't feel right until the guy was behind bars.

"What does he get out of bothering me?"

"He's just sick," Marie said. "Some people get off on behaving like that."

"How does he know what we do?"

"He doesn't. He watches me coming in the door and he makes it all up in his head."

Kelly snuggled up against Marie.

"How come you know so much?"

"I got an active imagination, that's all."

"Did you like doing it with Doug?"

"It felt good, but I never got off," Marie said. "I thought that was the way it was supposed to be till I learned to play with myself."

"Did you ever have those feelings for a girl?"

"Not really."

"You mean not until we got together."

"When we were in bed those first nights," Marie said, "it just seemed right. I didn't think about anything else."

"Me, too," said Kelly.

It turned out that the guy who harassed Kelly was sent to jail. It was all over the newspaper the next day. The judge had apparently decided that he was dangerous enough to be put away while awaiting trial. Kelly was glad her name wasn't mentioned, even though the article said he had been caught harassing a young mother in his own neighborhood. She hadn't told anyone at the GED class and none of the students even brought the subject up. Marie went out every day looking for work and Kelly got ready to take the tests.

One afternoon, just after Petey got back from day care, Kelly realized they were out of milk. She had put Petey down for his nap, but she didn't want to wake him up just to run an errand. Locking the door, she ran quickly down the street to Walgreen's. She grabbed the milk and a new copy of TV guide, zipped through the checkout line and started up the hill. When she got home she found the door open. She figured Marie must have come home while she was out. But when she called out no one answered.

"You home?" she called again.

The house was quiet. The kitchen was empty and no one was in the bathroom. Panicking she rushed into Petey's room. He wasn't in his crib. Kelly dashed back into the living room. Maybe Marie had come home and found Petey awake. Maybe she took him someplace with her. Otherwise how could the front door be open? She knew she'd locked it, she always did.

"Marie!" Kelly called out. "Petey!"

She looked everywhere for some sign that Marie had come home, a pocketbook, groceries, a six-pack. Nothing. Then she ran back into Petey's room.

"Oh, my God!" she screamed.

The drawers to Petey's little blue dresser were opened.

Someone had taken his clothing. His toys were gone, too. And in the closet where they left the car seat Marie had bought Kelly couldn't find it.

She ran screaming to the door just as Marie was coming up the stairs.

"He's gone," Kelly shouted. "Somebody took Petey!"

"What happened?" Marie asked, as she hugged Kelly to her.

"I went out for milk." Kelly was sobbing. "I only ran down to Walgreen's for a minute. I figured Petey would be okay. He's such a sound sleeper."

Kelly stood in the middle of the kitchen while Marie ran all over the apartment.

"Did you ask downstairs?" she said.

"I didn't have a chance. Besides, they come home late from work."

"His clothes are gone," Marie said. "Someone had to have gotten in here."

"I locked the door," Kelly said. "I remember locking the door."

Marie was on the telephone. Then she came back to Kelly.

"The guy's in jail, so it couldn't have been him who got in. But who—and why?"

"I don't know," Kelly wailed. "Oh, God. What have they done to Petey?"

The police arrived in seconds. They pulled up in two cruisers. Two cops came in while two others looked around the yard. They went up and down the street knocking on doors. Marie and Kelly sat on the couch.

Marie had her arm around Kelly. When Lieutenant Lombriglia got there he told Marie she'd better take Kelly up to the emergency room.

"She should probably see somebody," he advised. "Maybe get something to quiet her down."

Kelly sobbed softly as she tried to answer his questions.

Yes, she'd left the house, but just for a minute. She didn't even put the milk away. Of course, the door was locked. She made sure of that.

"It's been forced," one of the cops shouted to the lieutenant.

"Do you know anyone who might have done this?" Lt. Lombriglia asked.

"I don't know anyone except Marie," Kelly said. "Some kids in class, but they don't even know where I live."

Then Kelly looked at the lieutenant.

"Is Petey alive? What will they do to him?"

"We'll do everything we can to find him," he said.

Marie took Kelly to the emergency room where a social worker from the trauma team saw Kelly. The two women sat with her while Kelly tried to tell her what happened.

"I should never have left him," Kelly said. "I just know he's gone for good. I'll never see him again."

"The police will do everything they can," the worker said. "In the meantime, it's your job to take care of yourself."

"She's right," Marie said, holding Kelly's hand.

As soon as they got home Marie made Kelly take one of the pills the doctor in the ER had given her.

"You gotta get some rest," Marie said.

"I can't sleep until I know that Petey's okay."

"You won't be okay unless you do," Marie insisted.

They put the TV on, but the news reports of fires and missing children made Kelly think about Petey. She started to shake again and Marie held her tightly as they sat on the couch. All Kelly could see was Petey's little face in front of her, his shining brown eyes.

"My God, my God," she moaned. "Why did I leave him like that?"

"You only went out for a second," Marie reassured her. "And he was sound asleep. I know what a heavy sleeper he is."

Pretty soon Kelly felt tired. She couldn't talk, she couldn't even move. The last thing she remembered was Marie helping her into bed.

The next morning Lt. Lombriglia was at the door.

"I know it's early," he said to Kelly. "But I gotta ask you some more questions."

They went over every one of Kelly and Marie's moves up to the kidnapping. This was the first time the police had used that word. As soon as Kelly heard it she broke down.

"What about your parents?" he said to Kelly. "Were they over here last night?"

Kelly shook her head.

"They don't see her," Marie said. "They kicked her out when she got pregnant and she hasn't heard from them since."

"She didn't tell them what happened?"

"It didn't even come into my mind," Kelly said.

"They live here in town?"

"On Myrtle Square," Marie said

"Do you mind if I see them?" the lieutenant asked.

Kelly shrugged.

"If it would help," Marie said.

After the lieutenant left, Marie brought Kelly a cup of coffee.

"You should call Leanne and Earl," she said.

Kelly shook her head.

"They were probably waiting for me to screw up. Now that I've lost Petey they'll just say I told you so."

"We're gonna need all the help we can get to find him," Marie said.

Two hours later the lieutenant called. He told Kelly and Marie to come to the station immediately.

"Petey's dead. I just know he's dead," Kelly said as they ran down Elm Street toward the court house.

Marie kept her arm around Kelly all the way.

"If he was dead they'd have come to the house," she said.

When Kelly was shown into the lieutenant's office, she was shaking.

"I've got good news," the lieutenant told Kelly. "We found Petey at your parents'."

Kelly sat down hard.

"Is he okay? When can I see him?"

"He's fine," the lieutenant said.

Suddenly it came to her.

"You mean it was them? They came and took him?"

Lt. Lombriglia nodded.

"But they've never laid eyes on him!"

"It seems they've been watching you and Petey ever since you moved into Elm Street."

"They broke into my house! Why didn't they just call? I'd of let them see Petey."

"Apparently they didn't think you would."

"That's a crime what they did, isn't it?" Marie asked.

"Yes, it is," the lieutenant answered.

"I mean just breaking into the house like that and stealing Petey. Putting Kelly through all this."

"I'd say you're right," he said.

"Aren't you gonna do something about it? Shouldn't we make some kind of complaint?"

"I've charged them with breaking and entering and with kidnapping."

"Oh my God," Kelly said.

"They've responded that they had a right to take Petey because they are his legal grandparents. They've also charged you with being an unfit mother. They claim they came over for a visit. They said they knocked on the door and got no answer. When they heard Petey crying they forced the lock."

"Why didn't they just sit there and wait for me?" Kelly said. "For two years they don't see me. They never set foot in my house. All of a sudden I'm an unfit mother?"

"It seems they object to your relationship." He looked over at Marie.

"Marie's my friend," Kelly said. "When I was all alone she was the only one who cared about Petey and me."

"They're claiming it's bad for Petey to be brought up by two women."

"Marie's like another mother to Petey."

"You don't have to convince me," the lieutenant said. "But you may have to convince the Department of Social Services."

"They didn't call DSS!" Marie said.

"They've lodged a formal complaint," he said. "And they're keeping Petey until DSS investigates."

"I knew girls in the shelter who got reported," Kelly said. "But they didn't lose their children just like that!"

"Your parents have a lawyer who apparently convinced the department that Petey would be safer with them."

"They don't even know Petey!" Kelly shouted. "They've never laid eyes on him. He'll be scared without me. He's been with me every minute since he was born. He loves me. I've never done anything bad to him."

The lieutenant got up from behind his desk. He came over to where Kelly and Marie were sitting and he put his hand on Kelly's arm.

"Look," he said gently. "Petey's safe. I can't bring him back to you right now, but at least we know he's okay."

"What am I gonna do?" Kelly said. "When am I gonna see my son?"

"Hopefully DSS will give you some visitation while the case is pending. You'd better think about getting a lawyer."

"Kelly can't afford a lawyer," Marie said. "Between us all's we got is our checks."

That night Kelly cried herself to sleep. All she could think of was Petey in a strange house with Earl and Leanne. They had abused her. What would they do to Petey?

"We've got to call DSS," she had said to Marie before they went to bed.

The bell rang at nine the next morning. A DSS worker was at the door to interview Kelly. As she came in Kelly was glad that she and Marie had gotten up early to straighten out the apartment.

"I could go stay with my parents," Marie said as they made their bed together.

"I'm not going to lie about us," Kelly said. "We're together and that's that."

The worker, whose name was Janine, seemed nice enough. She asked the two women a lot of questions about Petey and Kelly tried to explain to her that Leanne had no business with her son.

"I mean they've never laid eyes on him," she pleaded.

"We understand that," Janine said. "But when someone makes a complaint we have to follow up on it."

"There was no abuse," Marie said. "Kelly never let Petey out of her sight except for that one time when she went out to get milk. If I'd of been here it would never have happened. I was out looking for work."

When the worker asked them how long they had been together, Kelly said, "Marie and I have been friends since first grade."

"When does she get her son back?" Marie asked.

"It depends on what the judge says," Janine replied. "You should know that your parents are going for custody. They'd like to adopt Petey."

After she left Kelly couldn't hold it in any longer.

"If they can take Petey from me I can get him back the

same way," she shouted.

Marie held her as they sat on the couch.

"Let's do it the right way," she urged. "We've gotta get some help."

"But who? Who?" Kelly was sobbing against Marie's chest.

That afternoon the Channel 5 news team was at the door. Kelly didn't want to let them in, but Marie said it might help to get their side of the story out. Jorge Quiroga interviewed them both as the cameramen moved throughout the apartment. They lingered particularly in Petey's empty room. When they wanted a shot of Kelly standing by the bed, Marie encouraged her to comply. Every time Quiroga mentioned Petey Kelly couldn't help crying.

The story appeared on the 11 o'clock news. Only Kelly and Marie were shown. Jorge told the TV audience that Kelly's parents had refused to be interviewed on the advice of their attorney. The story showed the two women sitting together on the couch. It showed Kelly standing next to Petey's crib. On the floor was his abandoned fire truck. Then Kelly was looking out the window

"All's I want is my son back," Kelly said as the camera focused in on her face.

The next morning, they heard a knock on the door. It was the two nuns from the group home in Danvers, Sister Rosina and Sister Beata Immaculata, only they weren't nuns anymore. Sitting together on Kelly's couch they explained to Kelly and Marie that they'd left the religious life a year before. They'd given up their orders and taken jobs in a new agency that worked with women who had been abused or lost their children to DSS. They went by their own names now.

"Just call us Rosie and Bea," Rosie said.

"We saw you on Channel Five last night," Bea said.

Marie turned to Kelly.

"I told you going on TV would help."

"Why don't you tell us everything," said Rosie.

Marie made coffee while Kelly showed the ex-nuns around the apartment. After Kelly and Marie had told their story, the two visitors sat quietly. There were both dressed in slacks. Rosie's gray hair was cut short. Bea wore hers in a loose ponytail.

"I'm sure you know we've been together for a long time," Bea said.

"We're here because we want to support you in your relationship," Rosie said. "Mostly though, we want to help you get Petey back."

"Don't you think we need a lawyer?" Marie asked.

"Of course you do," Bea said. "And we've got a good one for you. Gretchen's our staff attorney and she's a crackerjack."

"How can we pay her?" Kelly said. "They're telling us to find a public defender."

"Gretchen's services are free," Rosie said. "Why don't you plan on coming to Salem tomorrow so we can get the ball rolling."

After Rosie and Bea had left, Kelly fell back on the couch.

"To think that we used to make fun of them," she said. "I feel so guilty!"

"Don't let it bother you," Marie said, taking Kelly's hand. She kissed Kelly on the mouth.

"Is that what we have to call ourselves?"

"Lesbians, you mean?"

"I just never thought."

"Neither did I, but I love you," Marie said.

"I love you too."

Gretchen was great. In about fifteen minutes she had outlined a legal strategy that she felt would not only get Petey back but, in her words, would expose DSS for the fucked up bureaucratic mess it was.

She was big and blond with her hair flying out all around her face. She wore a gray pin-striped pantsuit and chain smoked Pall Mall Lites. Her office on Derby Street was stacked with case files. On her desk stood a personal computer with a yellow legal pad propped up between the keyboard and monitor screen.

The social worker had already done the intake on Kelly and Marie, so they got right down to business with Gretchen.

"If Bea and Rosie tell me you're great parents I'm ready to believe them," Gretchen said. "Besides, the case isn't really about that, is it?"

"I just want to know how Earl and Leanne can break into my apartment, kidnap my son and try to take him away from me," Kelly said.

"They obviously did it," Gretchen said. "The question is, do they get away with it? The bigger question is, do we allow DSS to place a child in what's effectively an alien environment? And moreover, do we allow that child who has had a stable home for most of his life to be traumatized by removal from that home and his mother's care?"

"All *right!*" Marie shouted.

Listening to Gretchen, Kelly felt better already. Gretchen suggested that they work with Lt. Lombriglia, who was clearly an ally.

"If we can help make those criminal charges against your parents stick it will support our case against DSS."

Gretchen said she would file an immediate motion in Superior Court to have Petey returned to Kelly and Marie pending the court's decision on the DSS complaints.

On the way back home Kelly and Marie talked excitedly about their visit to the agency.

"Do you think Gretchen's a lesbian?" Kelly asked.

"She had on a wedding ring."

"Don't you think women who live together wear them too?"

"Why not?" said Marie.

"Would you wear one with me?"

"Naturally."

"Let's get them," Kelly said.

After the excitement of meeting with Gretchen died down Kelly went into a slump. She missed Petey. She couldn't imagine that he'd be happy with Leanne and Earl. Besides, with both of them working who was taking care of Petey? She'd forgotten to mention this to Gretchen. Now she'd have to call her. It had to be an important factor in any decision about leaving Petey with her parents.

"Good thinking," Marie said, when Kelly told her she'd been back on the phone to Gretchen.

"Gretchen said she'd add it to the motion."

Marie slumped back on the couch with a beer.

"I had an interview at Store 24 today. As soon as the woman recognized me from TV she got standoffish. Can you imagine that? All they want is a stupid cashier!"

"When this is over—*if* it's over—let's go away someplace where we can start again," Kelly said.

"You mean move out of Gloucester?"

"Why not?"

"It never crossed my mind," Marie said.

"A lot of things never crossed my mind. But now they are."

Petey came home that night. The judge had ruled in Kelly's favor. Bea and Rosie picked Petey up at Earl and Leanne's. When Kelly opened the door and saw Petey in Bea's arms she broke down completely. Petey was overjoyed to see his mother. Sitting in the living room all four women passed him back and forth until he fell asleep in Kelly's lap.

"I don't think they're bad people," Rosie said of Kelly's parents. "It looks like they took good care of Petey. Leanne was in tears when she handed him to me. She had all his clothes washed and ironed. His things were carefully packed. They even bought him overalls and some new toys."

"Why didn't they just come and see him?" Kelly said.

"If they'd of called I would have let them visit Petey. He's their grandson after all."

Once the judge's decision hit the news, Kelly and Marie received calls of support from members of the North Shore Gay and Lesbian Alliance. They were invited to meetings and the group offered to hold demonstrations on their behalf when the custody case came to trial.

"They mean well," Bea said when Kelly called to ask what they should do. "But I think you and Marie are doing just fine by yourselves."

"Not without your help," Kelly said. "And please tell Gretchen again how much we appreciated what she's done."

"We're not through yet," said Bea.

After Petey came home, Marie got a job at Den-Mar nursing home in Rockport and Kelly went back to her GED classes. Marie loved working with the elderly. Every night she came home with stories about the little old ladies she helped bathe or whose hair she combed and brushed.

"I never did enjoy working in a factory," she told Kelly. "The nursing home is going to send me back to school so I can learn how to do rehab. My supervisor thinks I could be real good at OT and stuff like that."

"I'll get my GED and then we can go anywhere we want," Kelly said.

"Do we need to now?"

"Maybe not," said Kelly.

The custody case never went to trial. One day

Gretchen called.

"I just got off the phone with your parents' attorney," she told Kelly. "He's offered to drop his suit if you allow Leanne and Earl to see Petey."

"What do you think?" Kelly asked.

"They seem to have formed an attachment," Gretchen said. "Rosie told me how sad they were to give him back."

"Will they be good to him?"

"Having Petey in their lives might allow them to compensate for what they didn't give you."

"Do they want to see me?"

"Funny you should ask," Gretchen laughed. "They seem anxious to make it up to you."

Kelly was surprised.

"What do you suppose made them change?"

"It was you," Gretchen said. "They realized how much you'd fight to have your son back. That seemed to turn them around. They knew you loved Petey and they discovered how important Marie was to you."

"She comes with me," Kelly said. "If they want me and Petey they have to accept Marie, too."

"I think they will," said Gretchen.

That night Kelly had dinner ready for Marie when she came in the door wearing her blue uniform. It was a simple casserole with rice and chicken pieces. She poured a mix of Campbell's cheddar cheese soup and beer over the chicken like it said to do in one of her magazines. Then she put the casserole in a 350 degree oven to bake. She just had time to make a salad of iceberg lettuce and tomatoes before she heard Marie's key in the door. The minute

Petey saw Marie he let out a happy squeal.

Kelly and Marie sat down to eat with Petey between them in his high chair. Marie told them both about her day and Kelly reported that her tutor felt she was ready to start taking the GED tests.

"I've signed up to take math and social studies first," she said.

"You'll do great," Marie said.

"But I'm scared."

Marie leaned over to hug Kelly.

"After what you've been through nothing should faze you."

When Petey saw Kelly and Marie laughing, he started laughing too.

Later that night in bed, after they'd kissed and made love for the first time in a long time, Marie said, "Wasn't it funny about that crazy guy calling here all the time?"

"Seems like a million years ago," Kelly said.

"It does," Marie said. "But I was thinking it was those ridiculous phone calls that brought us together."

"He sounded like a very lonely person."

"I bet he's even lonelier in prison."

"I think Earl and Leanne were lonely, too," said Kelly.

"So was I," Marie said, hugging Kelly close.

Skag

For nearly ten years Jimmy Skag had been living at the homeless shelter. He wasn't destitute, and he really shouldn't have been homeless because he made good money when he was fishing. But Jimmy'd burned his bridges. Decades of doping had gotten him evicted so many times there wasn't a landlord in town would touch his case. Consequently, the neighbors got used to seeing his scruffy, yellow El Dorado on Main Street in front of the shelter. They'd given up complaining that he ought to be barred because he was gainfully employed. Although some still wondered why he couldn't afford sixty bucks a week for a room over Schooner's when it was apparent he was keeping that shit-can in gas.

But it wasn't that simple, as his high school classmate Tony Russo could tell you. Jimmy'd had the Virus for a long time. Now he was dying from it. Even the new protease inhibitors didn't make a dent in his condition. It was just a matter of time, his doctors said. Tony had prevailed upon Jill, the shelter director, to give Jimmy another chance, even though he'd been caught shooting up in the bathroom after everyone else had passed out from the booze or pills they managed to smuggle in.

Jimmy knew the cops felt better if they could keep an eye on him. And Tony, who'd finally convinced Jimmy to apply for Social Security Disability payments, had begged him to sign up for elderly housing even though Jimmy was only in his fifties.

"You can get in on a handicap," Tony had urged him. But the Housing Authority evoked his criminal record to keep him out, even though Jimmy hadn't had a conviction in years. Tony appealed the denial, persuading Legal Services to defend Jimmy. They were still waiting for a hearing date.

But these days Jimmy felt like shit. He was tall and lanky and he'd been strong all his life. Now he moved around in a sweat-stained T-shirt and blue jeans that were bagged out in the ass. Bent over, he shuffled up and down Main Street, coughing and hacking like a tubercular patient. While every other junkie in town was shitting the bed, Jimmy had kept himself going on a bill-a-day habit, which he dealt to pay for. That was when he was mobile. Most cops between Gloucester and Lynn were familiar with the yellow Caddie, although there were some in Lawrence or Lowell, who flagged him down just to bust his balls. Jimmy was cool, though. He'd pull over, get out of the car deferentially, and lean face forward over the hood while they patted him down. Then they'd kick back, all of them, and shoot the shit. Jimmy wasn't above informing on some of his buddies, especially those connections who copped him shit that had been adulterated.

So he survived. He dealt and fished his way through two marriages, a house mortgage, and a bunch of kids.

One son was dead from an overdose, another doing time for armed robbery. At least his daughters were straight. They were both married—Jimmy was four times a grandfather—and they'd taken him in from time to time.

But now it was a different story. Jimmy could barely get out of bed when the shelter staff called reveille each morning at six-thirty. And after a cup of coffee and a bowl of corn flakes, he could just about maneuver the first Camel of the day between his lips. He'd usually recruit someone else to drive his car, and they'd have a second breakfast at Dunkin' Donuts before they headed down to St. Peter's Park to catch the day's action.

Jimmy's real name was Mulcahey, James Ignatius Mulcahey. They'd called him Big Jim when he played backfield for Gloucester High. He could run like the wind and his passing had been legendary, though like many a schoolboy athlete, his life seemed to go downhill once he'd hung up his helmet and taken his last shower. As soon as he graduated Jimmy went fishing. He'd knocked up his girlfriend Karen. After a shotgun wedding there was little to do but follow his father and his grandfather on the sea. Those were the days of long trips with a lot of boozing before and after. By the time Jimmy got home to Karen, most of his share had been guzzled down at the Busy Bee or lost in all-night card games at the Elks Club. And what was there to come home to but crying babies and a wife who started complaining the minute she spotted his hungover mug at the door?

Forget getting laid, forget anything that might have brought you close once. Karen turned into a replica of her own mother. Fatter by the day, the two of them pissed their lives away gossiping on the telephone even though they practically lived next door to each other. Or the fucking bitch came over. She showed up whenever she felt like it, complaining about *her* old man, Karen's father, who spent his time ashore swapping war stories at the American Legion bar. When they weren't at Jimmy's house they were drinking coffee and complaining at Karen's grandmother's, dishes piled up in the sink, kids screaming to be changed or fed. That's when Jimmy realized it was a hell of a lot better to be at sea.

Fishing was only one kind of escape. The other consisted of booze or drugs. Jimmy's father was a boozer, so was Karen's. In fact, most of the men who fished out of Gloucester drank at one time or another. Booze seemed to be in everybody's blood in this shitass town. It was drugs that came later. Listen to some people, they'd tell you it was the foreign boats brought heroin into port. The big German freighters that unloaded at Vincent's Cove, starting in the Sixties.

But Jimmy knew better. Smack came in from Boston. That's where Jimmy had his first fix. When the boat he fished on used to take out at Commercial Wharf, the crew went down to a place on Columbus Avenue to drink and get laid. There were these black girls. Dance your ass off. Take you home and fuck you to death.

Jimmy made friends with one named Melanie. She was nineteen, two kids. Every time he was in port he gave Melanie a jingle and she'd be waiting for him. He'd pick up some steaks at Faneuil Hall, couple of bottles of Canadian rye, and head over for a night of balling. While Melanie got the kids into bed, or palmed them off on one of the neighbors in the project where she lived, Jimmy would make the drinks and broil the steaks. Sometimes they'd go out dancing at the Hi Hat, where the music was wild.

Jimmy and Melanie really hit it off. Jimmy even got tight with the regulars at the club. Offering him a toke right at the bar, they told Jimmy that he boogied like a brother. But after a few times together, Jimmy noticed something strange about Melanie. From the way her speech was slurred you'd think she was smoking too much weed. Even when she wasn't high she'd have trouble spitting the words out, or she'd start motor-mouthing. Then she'd fade wherever she was sitting. Sometimes she'd just crash.

One night after they'd made love, Melanie took an extra long time in the can. After she finally came to bed she seemed beyond tired. When Jimmy questioned her the next morning she looked at him slyly. And then she offered to let him try something she said was better than rye, better than anything they could smoke or sniff. Melanie had Jimmy sit at the kitchen table. She tied his upper arm with a garter. Producing a teaspoon, she put some white powder in the bowl and added a little water. She heated the spoon over the gas flame until the powder dissolved. Then she took an eyedropper with a hypodermic needle attached to it. Drawing the liquid up from the spoon with the bulb of the eyedropper, she came over to Jimmy.

"Just close your eyes, honey," she said, as she fingered the vein that bulged out in the crook of Jimmy's arm. Once she found it, all Jimmy felt was a tiny pinch as the needle entered. Then he saw a white flash across his eyeballs and something raced in his blood making him bob his head up and down as though he was listening to that hard bop they played at the Hi Hat, only there was no music, just some inner pulsation. After that he felt a sense of power and well-being as if nobody could reach him. And that was followed by an uncanny ability to concentrate for hours on the empty spoon Melanie had laid down on the table, the pores in the dark honey of her face, that crazy hair on the top of his hands.

Hours later, although it seemed like days, Jimmy came around. Melanie was there smiling at him.

"You feel like you died and gone to heaven?"

"I been someplace," Jimmy said groggily. "Someplace I liked."

Jimmy chipped for a couple of years. He never shot up at sea, only after a trip. And then the addiction set in. Anybody ask him why he had to have it, he'd just grin and say, "'Cause nothing makes me feel better." He couldn't be without heroin. He'd rather get high than go fishing. In order to maintain his habit he started to deal. That's when his friends started calling him Jimmy Skag. The minute he fell behind in his house payments, Karen's family turned against him. His father died and he begged every penny he could from his mother. Once he even stole her TV, selling it on the street because he was so desperate for a fix. Only his sister Agnes stood by him. Then she moved to Florida with her family. Still, she'd ask him down from time to time.

The years went by. Pretty soon no one would give Jimmy a site, even though they knew he stayed straight at sea. Captain's license or not, it was a sorry sight to see him on those gray afternoons drinking at the Old Timers' Tavern or the House of Mitch, reminiscing about the catches they once made on Georges or the Grand Banks before the government imposed those bullshit quotas, eventually closing some of the richest grounds to fishing.

Jimmy did some time, nothing serious, possession with intent to distribute. He never burned anybody. But he appeared sadder after he got out. And when his second wife Marilyn caught him in the sack with her best friend Lois, she threw him out for good. For a while he crashed on friends' couches. Once they caught him high or shooting up, he was out. When it got too cold to sleep in the car he'd head for the shelter.

At first it was a novelty, sleeping at a homeless shelter. The place was clean and it catered mostly to natives. If you got there by five o'clock, you could pick your own bunk. The food was good and you got to take a shower and wash your clothes. There was cable TV. They even let you smoke in the community room. It was like the Fishermen's Institute used to be in the old days when Jimmy would visit his uncle Everett who had a room there. After Urban Renewal came in, they tore the Institute down, evicting the few remaining mariners. Jimmy remembered the fight some people put up to save the old red brick building on Duncan Street; but like with most things that once mattered, people soon forgot it had ever existed. They forgot about the old seamen, too.

So Jimmy was now relegated to the shelter. And he was too sick to work. Jill pushed him to apply for General Relief while he was waiting for his disability award. Every morning he said he'd go down to the Welfare, which was just across the street from St. Peter's Park. But something would come up. There'd be some potent shit hit town. Or he'd drop by an old doper's pad, dozing the day away in front of the TV.

One night, while Jimmy was nodding over his plate at the dinner table, he got a call.

"Jimmy, youze okay?"

"Hangin' in," Jimmy said, recognizing the gravelly voice of his old skipper Captain Joe.

"Look, I got bad bronchitis. If I don't take the boat out by tomorrow I lose my days at sea. Then I hear they gonna close the grounds on us."

Jimmy usually fished with Joe. When they needed another crewman it was Jimmy's job to find someone.

"What you want me to do?" Jimmy asked Joe.

"You take her out, okay?"

"Me?"

"Yeah, you."

"Shit Joe, I'm sick, too," Jimmy shouted over the sound the TV.

"No, you can do it. You and two crew. She's all fuel up, ready to go. I stow some food in the galley."

"Joe, I can't!" Jimmy pleaded.

"Sure you can. Just think of your share if you have a good trip. There's cod, I hear. Don't pay no attention to those *fa'ngulos* at the National Marine. You go where we always go, you gonna get some nice groundfish for sure."

Then Joe hung up.

Jill, who had overheard the conversation, turned to Jimmy.

"Are you going to do it?"

Jimmy stuck another Camel between his lips, turning to the guy next to him for a light.

"Who'm I gonna get to go out with me?"

"Just look around you," Jill said.

"Gimme a break!"

"Chill out and listen." Jill pointed across the common room. Standing at the sink was a younger man with a pained expression on his bearded face.

"Not Shitter?"

"Why not?"

"Because he's worse off than me," Jimmy replied.

Shitter was the name they'd given this kid who had encopresis, a bowel disorder with alternating symptoms of constipation and incontinence. His father had the same problem. The two of them spent their lives shitting or worrying they were going to start shitting involuntarily. The doctors said it was probably genetic. Often just hearing that another person needed to shit or had diarrhea would cause both father and son to start shitting precipitously.

Shitter's father took Paregoric to control his bowels, becoming so addicted that he walked around in a daze for most of his life. As soon as he tried to break the dependency, he'd start shitting again. This made it hard for him to work steadily. And since he fished, no one would give him a site because they never knew if he'd start shitting just as they were hauling in the catch. The smell of his impacted feces was so bad it drove even the most hardened fishermen ashore.

Shitter had started with Kaopectate, working his way up to Imodium and Lomotil, and he'd learned to eat a lot of cheese to stay bound up. But once he discovered that heroin would constipate him, he started mainlining. It worked. But, like his father, he had to stay high to keep from shitting.

"Oh my fucking Jesus!" Jimmy gestured in Shitter's direction.

"He's a good fisherman," Jill said.

"Hey, I thought you'd be the first to tell me I was too sick to go out."

"Have you ever thought of taking one last trip?"

"I already took it." Jimmy laughed.

"Suit yourself," Jill said.

At two the next morning Jill woke Jimmy out of a sound sleep. She drove him and Shitter down to where the Lisa B. was tied. With them was Frankie Cucuzzo, who also happened to walk into the shelter the night before. Frankie had a panic disorder and he suffered from OCD. But when he took his meds he was a hard worker, although he could get compulsive about certain details, like how many steps it took to get in and out of the bathroom. Sometimes when he'd lost count he'd have to return and start over again, often re-washing his hands, or pissing one last time. The other guests would complain that between Frankie and Shitter, they could never get into the head when they needed to.

The story went that as a toddler Frankie's mother used to tie him in the back yard with a length of rope, just like a dog. That way she knew where he was and she didn't have to worry about him running away. But one day she apparently forgot he was out there. A ferocious storm came up with thunder and lightning. Poor little Frankie freaked out on his rope. Yelling and screaming for his mother, he stood in the middle of the yard while the rain soaked him to the bone. Terrified by the thunder, he crawled around looking for cover. When his mother, who spent most of her time on her knees saying the Rosary, couldn't locate Frankie in the house she called the neighbors who notified the police. As soon as the cops arrived, they found Frankie curled up under some bushes, shaking like a frozen animal. For weeks he didn't speak, and when he finally seemed to recover he would never let his mother out of his sight.

Captain Joe kept the Lisa B. tied up at the Marine Railways wharf on Rocky Neck. Built in Thomaston, Maine in 1949, she was an old side-trawler with a 165 horsepower engine, one of the last in the onshore fleet. Jimmy had taken her wheel many a time while Joe cooked or helped haul in the trawl, but he'd never skippered her. Still, he felt confident as Frankie cast off at 3 a.m. and they headed the Lisa B. out into the harbor to ice up at the Fort before starting for the fishing grounds.

The sky was clear and starry and the sea was calm. Just the same, Jimmy had the radio tuned into the weather channel. He decided to steer southeast for Stellwagen, or the Middle Bank, as the fishermen called it. It lay twelve miles off Gloucester, just about an hour and a half away at ten knots. Jimmy and Captain Joe had fished these small but once rich banks for years. Jimmy knew the best places by heart. Years before when he'd fished offshore, Jimmy began to learn about certain pet spots the skippers had, locations where their luck had been good or where they'd come to expect fish because the feeding conditions were exceptional. As a breeding area for sand eels, which the cod gorged themselves on, Stellwagen was no exception.

Jimmy approached the northeast corner of the bank. Although there was a slight roll to the sea it was otherwise calm. He shouted to Shitter and Frankie to get ready to set out the trawl. Throttling the engine, he gave the signal to begin lowering the big net assembly over the gunwales. First came the "codend" or bottom of the baglike trawl and finally the heavy mouth, which they managed to lower with the help of an overhead tackle, or jilson, and the winch. Once it touched the bottom of the sea, the mouth was held open while the trawl itself was steadied by a set of iron sheathed "doors," which were dragged along the bottom by towing cables attached to a set of metal straps.

Jimmy circled the vessel as the tide carried the net away from the boat before Frankie released the winch brakes. As the towing cable was paid out the doors would spread, dropping the net to the bottom. A tow of two or three hours would cover nearly nine miles of ocean bottom. Then the crew would usually haul back. Two or three sets, depending upon the catch and the weather, would make a trip, especially if they took in a near maximum catch of 10,000 pounds for each set.

From his post at the wheel in the pilothouse, Jimmy kept an eye on everything. Frankie and Shitter were doing what was expected of them. It was a little after six a.m. and they had the trawl under control. Jimmy held the Lisa B. to a towing speed of three knots. The sun had come up, flooding the ocean with light. Jimmy caught sight of a couple of other Gloucester vessels in the distance, but he decided not to contact them by radio. It was best to fish before the whale watchers, the chartered fishing boats and "booze cruises" began their tours, disrupting the peace and quiet of the ocean.

Shitter stood watch over the trawl, while Frankie paced the deck, stopping occasionally to scratch his neck. It was late September but the sun came up hot, climbing into a mackerel sky. Keeping an eye on the clouds, Jimmy listened to the maritime weather report, which was repeated every ten or fifteen minutes. At this time of year he knew that squalls were possible, even though the worst of the hurricane season was over. If it rained they usually continued fishing, especially if the hauls were adequate. It was better to tough it out once you were on the sea rather than to head for shore losing time and money. But a high wind was something else.

Once the engine began to labor, Jimmy figured it was about time to haul back. He'd had the trawls out for over two hours.

"Let's bring her back," he shouted to the two men, as he slowed the vessel down.

It was warm on the water, almost hot. Jimmy stripped off his flannel shirt, standing at the wheel in just a T-shirt.

Shitter and Frankie had their rubber overalls on, with knee-high boots. As the boat rolled with the swelling sea and the heft of the trawl on the way up, they steadied themselves simply by shifting their weight from one side of their bodies to another. Watching them, Jimmy admired their sealegs. Looking at these two *deficienti*, who would think that they had fished for most of their lives in that condition?

"Oh, wow! It's a big bag!"

Shitter hollered back to Jimmy as the winch ground and the trawl swung aboard, the dripping net swollen with fish.

"Jesus Christ!" Frankie shouted.

Jimmy came out on deck to help them.

"It's close to ten thousand pounds," he said, as the large cod spilled out.

"Who said this stock's depleted!" Frankie was jubilant.

"Only the government," Jimmy said, as they started to ice down the big fish.

Back in the pilothouse, Jimmy prepared for another set. He had that feeling that often came to him when a trip was going well, a feeling of being in control, even though more than thirty years on the sea had taught him you were never in control, just lucky. Yet for all that, this was the only time he could feel in charge without shooting up. It had been a matter of pride never to get high at sea, even under the most perilous conditions. The pressure of it kept him focused as though he was high.

Once they'd made the second set, Jimmy noticed a greater turbulence to the sea. It was clouding over, too, and he turned the radio up louder so he could hear the report over the steady thrumming of the engine.

The National Weather Service's announcer never betrayed emotion, even though he was reporting sudden squalls or outbreaks of rain in the Gulf of Maine. But Jimmy figured they'd be safe, at least for the second set. Experienced seamen as they were, he noticed Shitter and Frankie casting a glance at the ominous sky from time to time. Still, neither showed anxiety. They just kept their eyes on the towing cable as the engine began to labor, signaling to all of them that they had another full net.

"Let's haul!" Jimmy shouted as the wind bore down on them more strongly, bringing with it some big flying drops of rain.

Once they had the brimming net aboard Jimmy knew that it was time to head home. Back at the wheel, he brought the boat around carefully as Frankie and Shitter tended to the catch. Again he marveled at their calmness, even in the face of the rising wind and rain. But they stood fast, shoveling the cod into the hold and layering the big fish with ice before they hosed the deck down.

Two hours at most, Jimmy figured, and he would have them safely ashore. He wondered if, as captain, he should tell them that he hoped to outrun the storm. But he decided he'd only add to the pressure they must already feel. Better to keep them busy.

As they cruised shoreward, Jimmy reflected on the fact that Shitter hadn't seemed to make one move toward the head. And Frankie, while pacing a lot and sometimes rubbing his hands together, appeared just as calm as when they'd cast off. As for himself, Jimmy felt straighter than he'd felt since the year he'd spent in the slammer. Enforced sobriety hadn't been all that bad, he reflected. Neither had the big house. But Jimmy could always take care of himself. Except for the Virus. Whoever thought they were all sitting on a time bomb?

An hour off Eastern Point the rain hit, coupled with a blustery wind. Their work done, Shitter and Frankie stowed the net and secured the hatch covers. Then they joined Jimmy in the pilothouse.

"There's pizza from Valentino's in the cooler," Jimmy shouted above the sound of the wind and the steady electronic voice of the weather report. "Just throw it in the microwave. Or you can make some ham sandwiches if you want."

With the rain pelting the windshield of the pilothouse, Jimmy kept the Lisa B. on course. Even though it was early afternoon, the sky was dark. Huddling together in the comfort of the pilothouse, the three men munched on pepperoni pizza, washing it down with instant coffee that Shitter had quickly boiled the water for.

"This ain't that bad," Frankie said, tapping his fingers rhythmically on the compass glass.

"Hey, I been out in a lot worse," said Shitter.

"You guys did good," Jimmy said. "Made two sets, eighteen thousand minimum. At a buck a pound, add it up."

"There's our three shares," Frankie said, "and Captain Joe's. Then there's one for the boat."

"Hey, Jimmy, you can go see your sister in Daytona," Shitter said. "Spend the winter where it's warm."

"Wouldn't I like that!"

Reflecting on the rare occasions he'd flown south to be with Agnes and her family, Jimmy wondered if he had the strength to do it again.

He could hardly make out the Manchester shoreline through the rain. To starboard he caught Eastern Point Light as they slipped into the outer harbor.

"We're gonna make it!" Frankie shouted.

"Bet your sweet ass," said Shitter.

To leeward Jimmy made out the lights of a couple day boats. Each gave the other a blast of the horn. And Jimmy chimed in. Pretty soon they were back and forth on the radio as Jimmy rounded Ten Pound Island.

"How youze did?" It was Johnny Girolamo on the Katherine G.

"Made two sets. 'Bout eighteen, maybe close to twenty." Jimmy replied.

"Who said there ain't cod?"

That was Joey C. from the Joey C.

"The same *merdosi* who told everybody there was enough herring for the next hundred years!" Johnny laughed.

"*Fa'in cullo tutti!*" Joey said. "We're just doing what we gotta do before they close down the whole shootin' match."

As he listened to the banter over the radio, conversations he'd either monitored or took part in all his working life, Jimmy felt a great sadness coming over him. He knew he would never make another fishing trip. His fishing days as captain or crew were over, and his whole life on the water flashed in front of his eyes.

"Jimmy, you're okay. You're A-okay." Shitter was clapping him on the back while Jimmy steered the boat past the Paint Factory, heading her toward the State Fish Pier where they'd be taking out within minutes.

Frankie was jumping up and down.

"We made it! For sweet Jesus sake we made it!"

Jimmy saw himself as a teen-ager on his first offshore trip with the Favaloros. Somewhere there was a picture of him taken aboard the Carole and Gary a few years later, in a fleece-lined winter jacket, his hair in a Beatles cut. She was big, 425 horsepower, a wooden hull, built in 1945 in Boothbay Harbor. The Curcuru brothers had her. Then they sold her in New Bedford, where she was converted into a scalloper. That was twenty years ago. Who knew what her fate had been?

The fishing was good when he was a teen-ager just out of high school; it was still good when he was twenty-five. But if you knew the sea, like Jimmy and his father did, and you watched the fluctuation of the stocks, the *biomass*, as the National Marine Fisheries scientists liked to call it now, you could predict the bonanza that built a lot of big Italian and Portuguese houses and provided for the technology that allowed ambitious captains to locate and track their prey, would one day dry up.

The greed that drove the younger generation of fishermen eventually overtook them. These weren't your "highliners" of the great days of sail, who brought their catch in under the most daunting of conditions, pushing both men and ships to the breaking point. This was a younger breed who refused to listen to their fathers' counsel: "The house don't buy the boat—it's the boat that buys the house!" These guys wanted it all, the boat, the showy house, and the Cadillac (they also wanted to get laid outside their marriages). When the stocks began to collapse, first in the Sixties and later and more severely in the Seventies and Eighties, they weren't squeamish about diversifying. They got into dope running; and when that got too hot, they did the unthinkable—at least for their fathers and their *nonni*—they sunk their boats for the insurance money.

The boats and their crews passed in front of Jimmy's glazed eyes: Cape May, Santa Lucia, Santa Maria. Jimmy had always favored the Italian boats. Even if he was an Irishman, they always said he was a Guinea at heart. He even looked like one! Who knows, maybe somewhere in his family, deep in his blood, there had been a Sicilian.

He'd fished on the St. Rosalie, out of Rockland and Gloucester. Then there was the St. Jude, the Serafina N., Joseph and Lucia, Our Lady of Fatima, Last Chance. Name the boats, Jimmy had fished on them all. And most of them were gone now. Sold, sunk, or retrofitted for lobster dragging on the ocean floor, once the quotas limiting each boat's catch had been imposed, along with the seasonal closures of fishing grounds. Or just lost, like the men themselves.

You didn't know if they were dead or not. You'd miss them. Someone would claim they'd gone looking for a site in Portland or New Bedford. Maybe you'd run into them drinking at the Old Timers' Tavern. Quietly they'd left fishing. They were silk screening T-shirts in the industrial park, or they'd taken early retirement, eking out an existence in rooming houses or at the "Y" on veteran's benefits or Social. But they were gone from fishing. They never showed their faces again on the waterfront, never even joined the other fishermen lounging on the wooden benches behind St. Peter's Club. It was as if they were dead to the sea, having turned their backs on it, or more rightly, having been driven from the calling their fathers had taken up from their own fathers and grandfathers.

As he brought the Lisa B. alongside the Fish Pier he wondered where it would all end. But he didn't have time to follow the thought through. As soon as Frankie had jumped on the dock to tie up and start taking out, Captain Joe came aboard. And Jimmy looked up to see Jill, smiling down at him, Shitter and Frankie.

"Oh, you done good!" Captain Joe said, shaking Jimmy's hand. "I tol' you you'd be okay."

Once Shitter and Frankie started celebrating their success, deckhands from the other boats shouted back. Jamming their fists into the air, they gave Jimmy and his crew the high sign.

"Fuck the government!" someone yelled. "The fishermen know the sea!"

Back at the shelter Jill had prepared a turkey dinner. Showered and wearing clean clothes, Jimmy, Shitter and Frankie sat grinning while the other guests sang their praises. Outside, a northeaster raged. Rain beat against the windows and the wind shook the converted 19th-century house, rattling the doors as though someone was desperately trying to get in.

Jill poured everyone a glass of non-alcoholic champagne.

"Here's to our guys!" she said, raising her cup. "Home safe with a big trip!"

"Hear! Hear!" the homeless men and women shouted, as they all tipped their glasses back.

Jimmy was the last to go to bed that night. Usually he couldn't keep his eyes open. But after they'd shut the TV off and everyone else had turned in, he and Jill sat up talking over coffee.

"I don't feel a bit tired," he said.

"Must be all that adrenaline."

"Can you believe Frankie? He was like a rock the whole trip!"

Jill shook her head in sympathy and amazement.

"And Shitter never once used the head!"

"They knew you and Captain Joe were counting on them," Jill said. "And they didn't want to let you down."

"Well, they didn't. That's for sure."

Jimmy lit up again.

"I think I'm going to Daytona for the winter."

"Your sister will be glad to see you," Jill said.

"I may not be back."

"We'll miss you."

Jimmy looked hard at Jill.

"I don't want to die in Gloucester."

Jimmy's eyes wandered around the room he'd talked, eaten and smoked in for the past ten years. Over in the corner was the VCR that had to be chained to the wall so no one would steal it. The battered coffee urn sat on the counter next to the stove, twenty clean mugs lined up for breakfast the next morning. He gazed, as if for the first time, at the oil paintings on the walls, pictures of the waterfront as it had once looked, jammed with fishing vessels, salt cod drying on wooden stages. A vagrant artist, once a fisherman, had done the paintings, leaving them to the shelter after he died. Like with Jimmy, the shelter had become his final refuge.

"I do and I don't," he said.

"I know what you mean." Jill reached across the table for Jimmy's rough hand. And Jimmy gripped hers tightly in return.

"I think I'm goin' right away. Can you get me a plane ticket? I'll have the cash when we settle tomorrow."

"No problem," Jill said.

As Jimmy lay in his bunk listening to the heavy breathing of the other homeless men around him, he wondered how he'd gotten himself and the others out to sea and how he'd managed to keep them there while they fished. It seemed as though another person had achieved it, bringing Frankie and Shitter safely to port before the big storm hit. But Jimmy knew it had been him. And he was happy he'd been able to do it.

He was ready to die now, whenever death would come. But he didn't want to die in a shelter or in the hospital. He wanted to die at home, even if he didn't have a real one anymore. His sister would give him a home, and a bed to die in. She was the only family he had left and he looked forward to the rest Agnes had been promising him.

As he lay quietly, waiting for sleep to overtake him,

Jimmy understood that some things were finished. He wouldn't fish again and he was finally through with heroin. In that luminous moment on the rolling sea, while he watched the two men working their hearts out, for him and for themselves, he realized how much he'd lost, literally thrown away, for the illusory power that skag had held out to him. Who knows what he might have achieved without it, what kind of captain he might have become?

There would be time to think about all that. But now the job was to get himself onto that plane for Daytona. He could count on Jill to buy him a one-way ticket. And he knew she'd offer to drive him to Logan airport. But he needed all the strength and willpower he could muster to get aboard, to deliver himself to his sister. Once he was in Agnes' hands, he could let down a little. Once he was home, things would be different.

Still, it had been wonderful at sea, even for just a day! It had been heaven. But Jimmy had been too busy paying attention to the weather and the boat to even think about the pleasure he'd always taken from being on the water. Maybe he could now. Maybe if he got himself to Daytona everything else would follow.

◇

The Psych Unit

As soon as Rochelle came on duty, she heard that Terrence had been admitted during the night. It wasn't the first time he'd OD'd, the head nurse on the psych unit reminded her, and it wouldn't be the last.

"What's Amanda think, I was born yesterday?" Rochelle muttered to herself as she rushed onto the ward where they held the drug cases before remanding them to detox.

Terrence was asleep, or out of it. She couldn't tell. All she could see was his long stringy hair spread out on the pillow and his face that seemed to have a permanent tan. It was as though he'd just come back from 'Nam, the place he once told Rochelle he only went to get high.

"No way did I do two tours in that shit hole out of patriotism," he said. "It was dope that drew me every time." Then he'd chuckle reflectively.

"My sweet loving balls! Were we ever shitfaced! Did we get fucked up!"

And then maybe he'd pull a couple of grease-stained Polaroids out of his wallet and stick them up at Rochelle as if she hadn't seen them before.

"Them's my two buddies, and that's me."

The images of Terrence were of a youth barely out of high school, skinny and wild faced. His companions were black, with enormous Afros, their fatigues drenched with perspiration.

Rochelle had come to understand that wasn't the real Terrence. It was one of the faces he liked to show, one of his many defenses, as the unit shrink was fond of reminding them at supervision. But it wasn't the Terrence she knew.

"I heard you were back," Rochelle said, automatically reaching out to take his pulse.

"Oh, it's pumping, sweetie pie. Ol' heart's still beating." Rochelle smiled.

"Lie still so I can get a reading."

"I can't lie any stiller, they got me strapped down to this fuckin' bed!"

There was no use asking Terrence why he continued to abuse himself. Rochelle had spent enough time with junkies to know the answer. It was ridiculous to wonder why he didn't value his own life more. He'd told her outright that he didn't care if he lived or died.

"Hey, who's gonna miss ol' Terrence?"

"A lot of people," Rochelle had answered. "What about your daughter?"

"I been dead to Charmayne since she was born."

What could you say to that? Besides, it wasn't Rochelle's job to talk this way with Terrence. She wasn't his therapist, she was only a psych nurse. She was encouraged to relate to the patients, to be part of their treatment team. But mostly she was there to see that he took his meds and didn't try to leave the ward.

Rochelle had been at the hospital for nearly a year.

During that period Terrence had OD'd at least three times. And once before he'd slashed his wrists. The first time they met he rolled back his pajama sleeves revealing deep, white longitudinal scars. It was lucky his girlfriend had found him when she did. But Roberta was gone now. Unable to help him stay straight, she took off with their daughter. Last anyone heard she and Charmayne were in St. Paul, where Roberta had family.

Coming back home was like deja vu for Rochelle. Sometimes she wondered why she'd talked Larry into selling their condo, uprooting Tiffany and little Larry, to return to a place that never changed. Or was it the people? Rochelle had graduated from UNH with high honors. She had a BS in nursing and soon she became an RN with a psychiatric specialty. She had a good job in Durham, where they lived and the kids went to school. And Larry was doing really well in software sales. They'd even planned to build a house in Newmarket.

But one day Rochelle woke up with Gloucester on the brain. The city she and Larry had been born in and where Tiffany had gotten her start in school seemed to be calling to her. She'd read in the Boston Globe classifieds that the hospital was looking for a psych nurse. Rochelle applied and got the job. The pay was slightly better than what she earned at St. Jude's, but it was the chance to go home that decided the issue for her.

Things were going well for Rochelle and the family that meant so much to her. She loved Larry even more now than when they'd first met at night school. He'd been with her every step of the way through college, baby-sitting when she needed to study or take an evening course, helping to pay tuition. And Larry, little Larry and Tiffany were at the stadium when she graduated *summa cum laude*. As soon as her name was called to come and receive her degree, they all jumped up and started to cheer.

"I knew you could do it," Larry said.

Rochelle loved nursing. She loved the hard work of it and she enjoyed the contact with patients. She had always been interested in what made people tick, and now, working on psych wards, she began to observe in actuality a lot of what she'd only read about in textbooks.

The psychology courses had been her favorites, especially abnormal psych. She had read way beyond the assigned medical texts, digging into Freud and Jung in the library stacks, absorbing case studies of anxiety and depression as if they were stories or novels. She'd studied Karen Horney on the etiology of neurosis and Anna Freud on the ego and its defense mechanisms. She'd been particularly moved by Alice Miller's writings on childhood abuse.

Her teachers teased her that psychoanalysis was passé, that the answer to what made people who they were was in the human brain and nervous system. We're the products of our own biochemistry, our DNA, they lectured. Even delusions were now thought to have a biological or biochemical basis. Rochelle didn't disbelieve that. But there was something in depth psychology that drew her. Learning about how others experienced and confronted their pain and fears—or fled them—she learned more about herself. And that was deeply satisfying.

Working now and coming home to Tiffany and little

Larry she had less time for reading. But she got a lot out of supervision and from attending case meetings. When Dr. Byron, the unit psychiatrist, complimented her on her insights, Rochelle left the meeting feeling like she did when one of her teachers had praised her.

But now she was confronted by Terrence who was back on the ward, more suicidal than ever. He'd refused detox at Bedford Veteran's Hospital, shouting that he was sick and tired of helping doddering old vets get around in their wheelchairs.

"I ain't sitting in front of no TV with those Thorazine zombies! All them fuckheads in paper slippers drooling into their laps!"

Rochelle almost laughed. Terrence had a way of describing a scene so that its inherent absurdity was revealed. And he was more articulate than you might think, listening to him shoot his mouth off. When he was out of sight of the therapists, who were always trying to rope him into attending group, he'd look Rochelle in the eye and comment quietly, "You know I'm not insane, and it's not just PTSD that I'm suffering from. I'm really tired of living."

"Don't you think that's depression?" Rochelle asked.

"You know it is," Terrence answered sadly.

Then he'd ask her not to leave so soon or to help him sit up so that he could give himself a shave.

"You sure you don't want a little hair cut, too?"

"I'd be like Samson without my hair."

"But I'm not Delilah!"

"No, you're prettier," he laughed.

Rochelle knew that Terrence wasn't about to go back

on Methadone, much less undergo ECT again. He'd told her that he hated the clinic, he hated being under the gun each day, taking the drink at a certain hour, pissing in a jar: group therapy, individual counseling, meetings.

"I'm too old for that regimentation. Besides, I lived through it once in the army. Never again, I promised myself."

"Vietnam sure didn't sound that way," Rochelle said.

"Hey, 'Nam was different. Once you were in country it was every man for himself. Fuckers went into the jungle, they never came out. Or if they did, they were so stoned you didn't recognize them. Or maybe you found them ball-less hanging out of a tree."

Rochelle knew very little about the war in Vietnam. They'd done a unit on it in current events class in high school. And she remembered watching a series on Southeast Asia on public television that had some graphic footage of the massacre at My Lai.

Terrence's addiction and his suicidal tendencies had all been attributed to post traumatic stress as a result of his service in Vietnam. Supervision or treatment meetings focused on trying to help him deal with that in therapy. The plan Dr. Byron proposed involved getting the heroin under control. Once that was achieved, it was felt that Terrence's depression might manifest itself more dramatically for treatment. In the end, not a lot of hope was held out.

Amanda, who'd known Terrence ever since the unit had been opened, predicted that he would eventually kill himself.

"He'll tell you himself that he doesn't want to live."

"But he's still alive," Byron disagreed. "There's a will to survive that's stronger than the will to annihilation. Besides, I see the suicidal mode, the threats to kill himself, the despairing talk, as a defense against his pain."

"Isn't that the typical self-indulgence of druggies?" one of the therapists asked.

Rochelle sat listening to the exchange. She wanted to participate, but she held back, afraid that the others might resent her speaking up, especially Amanda, who was always making wisecracks about Rochelle's concern for Terrence. "I've been wondering," she began. When the others' eyes were turned on her, she froze for a second. "Do you think that the trauma we've been treating Terrence for, I mean the primary one, comes from his experiences in Vietnam? Maybe he was traumatized long before he left the country?"

"What are you suggesting?" Byron asked.

"He shows a lot of the signs of a person who was abused in childhood," Rochelle said. "I mean, Alice Miller says—"

Amanda rolled her eyes.

"Go on," Byron urged Rochelle. "I think Alice Miller's work is entirely apposite here."

"Miller says that one trauma can mask another, and that the trauma one initially presents, dramatic as it may seem, can often be a screen for more primal pain."

"Aren't we reaching a bit?" Murray, the skeptical therapist asked.

"Not at all," Byron said. "Let's explore for a minute what Rochelle is suggesting."

"His father was an alcoholic," Rochelle offered. "He also fought in the Second World War, where he was badly wounded."

"What else?" Byron asked.

"He was a fisherman. He was lost at sea."

"How do you know this?" Amanda asked. "It's not in Terrence's records.

"I know it from growing up here," Rochelle insisted. "My grandmother knew his mother. The husband beat her and the kids constantly. He beat Terrence so badly once that he was thought to have incurred brain damage."

"That's anecdotal," Murray interjected. "What does Terrence say about his childhood? What does he remember of it?"

"It's not what he remembers," Byron said. "It's what he's denied!"

Rochelle knew something else, too, although she decided not to share it. She remembered Dot her grandmother saying that Terrence's father used to warn Terrence and his little brother Billy that if they misbehaved while he was out fishing he'd punish them severely when he came ashore. He threatened to tie them to the railroad tracks near their house, and one time he actually did it to Billy. The neighbors never forgot that night because they heard Billy's screams for help as the Rockport train approached the Maplewood Avenue crossing. Then the little boy's shrieks were drowned out by the whistle of the train, the rumbling of the cars on the tracks. After the train had left, someone sneaked over. Billy was gone. It turned out Terrence had rescued him, risking the beating from his father he knew would follow. But Billy was never the same after that. He hardly spoke. When he was twelve years old he shot his best friend on Dogtown, leaving the body in a shallow grave.

Rochelle knew these things and just to dredge them up brought her great sadness. She had wished she could discuss them with someone on the staff.

Abruptly Terrence signed himself out. He was gone by the time Rochelle arrived at work.

"Fat lot of help your Alice Miller's given him," Amanda commented after she told Rochelle the news.

"I never said it would," Rochelle sighed. "I was just trying to understand what drives him."

"The same thing that drives all these junkies," Amanda retorted, "the next fix!"

Rochelle gazed steadily at Amanda.

"I don't believe it's that simple."

"Then you'll never get anywhere in this work."

When Rochelle knocked on the door of Dr. Byron's office, she was still unsure about discussing Terrence with him.

"Come in," Byron said looking up. When he noticed it was Rochelle he smiled.

"I'm sorry to bother you, doctor."

"Please call me Jack."

The doctor was young, probably in his late thirties or early forties, although his thick brush of mustache made him look older. With his neatly pressed gray flannels and a herringbone jacket he looked more like one of Rochelle's professors than a busy hospital psychiatrist. But Rochelle liked it that he paid attention to the way he dressed. Most of the caseworkers looked like they'd just come in from jogging. Byron's clothing added to his dignity. Still, he was open and friendly.

"I wanted to talk about Terrence," Rochelle began.

"You must be disturbed that he's signed himself out again."

"I feel there's more we could have done."

"We or you?" Byron said, smiling again.

"Me, I guess."

"I know what you mean," he said kindly. "Every time someone terminates treatment prematurely we feel responsible. We feel we let them down. We feel let down ourselves."

"That's exactly my situation," Rochelle said.

"Let me tell you, I feel the same way. Whenever I lose a patient I feel it's my fault, even though I know there are often the most objective reasons behind the patient's flight—resistance, fear, anger."

"That helps me feel better," Rochelle said.

"Well, you should feel better because you've worked hard with Terrence. You've gone beyond what your job description mandates. And I'm not saying that critically."

Rochelle suddenly found tears in her eyes.

"You have a great advantage in understanding a patient like Terrence," Byron said. "One of the reasons we welcomed you here was that you're a native and you grew up in the culture we mostly serve. I hope you don't mind my acknowledging that."

"Sometimes I feel looked down on," Rochelle said. "I

mean, some of the other staff—"

"I know what you're saying and I'm sorry for that. You're a highly qualified RN. And you must know that we hired you for your abilities as well as for what we felt were your potential insights into the lives of our patients. I personally love it that you've read in psychoanalytical literature."

"My teachers laughed at me for it."

"Some day you may have the last laugh," Byron said. "Clinical fashions come and go, but there are essential insights into what makes us human, insights that didn't begin with Freud but that he was able to synthesize. Others have carried his work forward, adding creatively to it. The human personality isn't static, it evolves. The self is gained not created, or acquired like a commodity."

Pushing his chair back against the wall, Byron propped his foot up on the desk. "In my view a psych unit should be a place of learning, for the staff as well as for the patients. I'm going to do something about that."

"I've already learned a lot," Rochelle said.

"It's because you're open to it. Don't ever lose that openness. It will make you a better clinician. I dare say, you'll be a better person for it, too."

"What am I going to do about Terrence?" Rochelle asked.

Byron touched the fingers of both hands together. Staring down at his hands, he bowed his head until Rochelle could see the soft part in his thick brown hair.

"Try to stay involved but uninvolved," Byron explained. "I call it walking a line. Be there for Terrence but understand that you can't *be* Terrence. And when he falls down, as he will, don't feel that you've let him down."

Dr. Byron was smiling as Rochelle backed out of his office.

"Oh, wait!" he said, pushing his chair against the wall as he jumped up.

"You were right on target with Alice Miller. You might also want to take a look at James Chu's work on trauma and dissociative disorders."

As Rochelle made her way past the nurse's station she noticed that Amanda was giving her the eye. She'd obviously watched her coming out of Byron's office. Rochelle decided to say nothing. She wouldn't give Amanda the satisfaction of getting to her.

Why does she have to be that way? Rochelle wondered. I've done nothing to her. I've just tried to do my job as well as I can. Maybe that's the problem, she decided.

At home over the weekend Larry noticed that she was preoccupied. Once little Larry was in bed on Saturday night, he came to sit next to Rochelle on the couch. The TV was going softly, but neither of them was watching the screen.

"I know you're worried about something," Larry said.

Rochelle let him take her hand. She'd been wishing he'd come and join her. Tiffany was out on a date and that made Rochelle pensive. She was already applying to colleges. What would she do when her little sister left home for good?

"Is it about work?"

"It is and it isn't," Rochelle said. "I mean it's about a lot of things."

"Not about us, I hope." Larry looked concerned.

Rochelle squeezed Larry's hand.

"I never worry about us."

"But I worry about you," Larry said. "Sometimes you take the world's cares on your shoulders."

"I've always been that way, haven't I?"

"For as long as I've known you."

"I can't seem to stop."

"I don't want you to stop," Larry said. "Maybe just lighten up a bit. I was thinking we haven't taken a vacation for a long time."

"Washington was the last time, with the kids," Rochelle recalled. "We did have a good time though."

"Maybe it's time for just you and me to go away, even for a weekend. Tiffany's old enough to take over."

Rochelle felt herself resisting. She was about to tell Larry that it wasn't the right time, that she didn't feel up to going away, that she was really worried about leaving Tiffany in charge, when a thought crossed her mind.

"The only time we've ever been alone together was when we first started going out," she recalled.

"I've been thinking about those times."

"It's like we've suddenly gotten older. You go to work and come home. I go to the unit every day. And around us the kids are growing up."

That night in bed, after Tiffany had come home and her room was still, Rochelle snuggled against Larry.

"Let's make love like we used to," she said. "I want you so much."

Later they lay naked in each other's arms. Rochelle had wiped the tears of release from her eyes. And after whispering into her ear that he loved her, Larry had dropped off to sleep. The last thing that Rochelle had said to him was, "Let's go somewhere together, just you and me."

When Rochelle arrived at work the next morning the unit was eerily quiet, the nurse's station deserted. Patients who usually greeted her sat silently smoking in the nearby lounge. As she approached the coffee room, where staff often congregated, Rochelle heard the murmur of voices.

"You'd better sit down," a red-faced Amanda said as Rochelle entered the room. "Who's gonna tell her?"

"I don't know if you've heard the news," Murray said as he moved his chair closer to Rochelle's.

"What news? What's going on?"

Rochelle could feel panic rising in her body

"Something terrible's happened," Murray said.

Rochelle felt herself wanting to hear and resisting at the same time. In the space of the small room Amanda and the other clinicians loomed like so many of the people from her past who had brought her bad news.

"Jack Byron was killed last night."

Rochelle held her breath.

"How? Where?"

Murray stretched his hand out to touch Rochelle's.

"Hit and run on Nugent's Stretch," he answered quietly. "Jack was on his way home late. He'd driven in from Rockport to see a patient who tried to hang herself. He was alone in the car. Suddenly some guy in a pickup appeared out of nowhere. Apparently he'd been driving erratically. His truck careened across the lanes, hitting Jack's car head on."

Rochelle could barely take the information in. All she could picture was the doctor sitting at his desk the day they'd talked, the deep part in his carefully brushed hair.

"The police flew him to Mass. General in a helicopter," Murray continued. "But Jack died on the operating table. The head injuries were massive."

Rochelle shook her head back and forth as if the motions would make her feel better.

Those in the room added what they knew:

The person who hit Byron left the scene of the accident. He abandoned his truck and ran into the woods. A passerby who'd witnessed the accident and stopped to help ran after him. Another witness called the police on his cell phone. Others joined in the pursuit. By the time the police had arrived, those who'd chased the driver of the pickup found him cowering behind a stone wall. The police took him into custody. He'd been on probation. The truck was stolen.

"It was Brucie McCoy," Amanda said.

Rochelle recognized the name of one of the city's most notorious drug dealers.

"He was high as a kite," Amanda continued. "Kept asking the police when he could leave. He didn't even know what he'd done!"

Rochelle got through the day by an effort of will. She heard herself speaking to her patients as though eavesdropping on a TV talk program. The entire unit was in a trance, including the staff. Patients who were often contentious or unruly were merely sullen. A couple of the social workers in the supervision group suggested getting the staff together to try to process what had happened, but with Dr. Byron dead they had no one to lead the discussion.

"Who can talk at a time like this?" Sue, the other MSW said. "I can't even think."

The memorial service two days later at Temple Ahavat Achim was packed. Rochelle had never been to the synagogue on Middle Street. No one from the unit had asked her to accompany them, so she sat alone near the rear of the sanctuary listening to the mournful voice of the cantor.

The entire hospital staff was there, including every doctor she knew. She recognized some city officials from their pictures in the newspaper. And Tony from the Welfare office was sitting across from her. There were even some of Jack's patients who'd been allowed to leave the unit for the service. In front sat an attractive dark woman with a little boy at her side. Rochelle thought they must be the family.

Several people spoke eulogizing Jack, including the chief of staff at Addison Gilbert and a soft-spoken gray-haired man, who introduced himself as a colleague and friend of Jack's from Boston.

"I've never worked with a more committed therapist," he told the mourners. "I cannot begin to tell you what a loss it is to the profession of healing."

At those words Rochelle began to shake. She put a handkerchief to her face, sobbing into it. She thought she would cry her heart out and she wondered what those around her would think. But others were similarly moved and it seemed a long time before the members of the congregation began leaving row by row. When she looked for Tony he was gone.

Rochelle felt the need to speak to Jack's widow and son. That night, after little Larry was asleep and Tiffany had gone into her room to do homework, Rochelle wrote to her.

A week later Rochelle received a note from Jack's wife, whose name was Miriam. She had written it on a card that reproduced a painting of "Fresh Water Cove" by Fitz Hugh Lane. The handwriting was compact and neat.

"Jack spoke warmly about you," Miriam wrote. "I wish you'd come and see me."

The next day Rochelle knocked on the door of a small, brown-shingled cottage on Marmion Way. Even though Rockport was just a few miles from Gloucester, she'd only been there once or twice. Still, its neat clapboard houses and narrow streets made her feel as if she were back in New Hampshire.

Miriam answered the door. With her dark eyes and lustrous hair she looked more beautiful than she'd appeared to be in the synagogue.

"Please come in," she urged, giving Rochelle a hug.

The two women sat drinking tea while the little boy played quietly with his toys in the other room.

Miriam shook her head.

"He's still waiting for his father to come home. I just don't know what to tell him."

Rochelle felt a catch in her throat as she tried to speak.

"You were very kind to invite me, Mrs. Byron—"

"Please call me Miriam. I feel I know you, listening to Jack talk about you and some of the other people on the unit."

"We miss Jack. It's not the same there without him."

"Jack loved the unit. He seemed to have found himself working with all those drug addicts and alcoholics."

Miriam lowered her voice.

"I feel completely abandoned. I'm a suburban girl from Long Island. I never wanted to come here in the first place. I just couldn't relate to Gloucester. Bump into someone at Star Market and they tell you their life's story. It was too much for me, people in your face like that. Jack thrived on it. He was dying to live in the heart of town. I had to drag him away from a house he fell in love with on Portuguese Hill! We compromised by moving here."

"Rockport's certainly not as raucous as Gloucester," Rochelle said. "Just compare the police notes."

"I must sound bitter. Please forgive me. I loved Jack desperately. I would have done anything to make him happy. I just don't know what I'm going to do with my life. I used to work at the Whitney in New York. I could go back. But I have to stay here until the trial—"

Miriam covered her face with both hands.

"I can't comprehend it," she sobbed. "My husband, obliterated while he was on his way home to us. Killed by some totally useless degenerate! It's so abrupt, so cruel!"

Rochelle wanted to get up and put her arms around Miriam. Instead, she reached across the narrow space between them and grasped Miriam's hands. She noticed Miriam's tasteful dark dress and she looked around the room at the beautiful antiques, the stuffed bookcases, paintings on the wall. In the next room she heard the little boy murmuring over his trucks, singing softly to himself.

"I lost my father when I was a little girl," Rochelle began. "The police killed him. And my baby brother Matty died in his crib. My mother was homeless. She froze to death in an abandoned warehouse. My parents were both junkies. So was Roy. He was the father of my little sister. Tiffany was all I had. There was nothing I wouldn't do to protect her. One night Roy tried to take her away from me and I stabbed him in the throat. I was glad I did it. But killing Roy didn't bring anybody back."

Miriam had stopped crying. Her eyes seemed to be searching Rochelle's face.

"I'm married now," Rochelle said. "I love my husband and my son. My sister still lives with us. She's a senior in high school now. I tell myself I'm happy. I feel happy a lot of the time. But deep down I'm still lonely. I miss my father and my mother. My grandmother's gone, too. I'm a lonely person and I don't think I can ever erase that feeling."

Miriam gripped Rochelle's hands more tightly.

"I don't know how much Jack knew about your history," she said. "But I can tell you that he admired you."

Miriam sat back, her eyes wet with tears.

"Jack was hesitant to share information about his analytical training. But I can tell you that he'd completed all the requirements of a candidate at the Boston Psychoanalytic Society—the theoretical work, a training analysis with Dr. Cavitch, who spoke at the memorial, the supervised analysis of his own patients. He was about to become certified as a practicing analyst and he was so proud of himself."

"I wish I had known," Rochelle said. "I really respected him."

"His colleagues here made fun of him. They said it was regressive to become an analyst. They told him he'd be undermining a brilliant career in psychiatry, that people would consider him a quack."

"I don't believe that!"

"Jack persisted. It took nearly ten years and a lot of money we didn't have. Once he'd been certified his plan was to find a niche for himself in the analytical community, even if it meant giving up his job at the unit, which he loved. He wanted to see a few patients and write, maybe teach a little. He dreamed of a quiet retreat, away from what he thought was the madness of this life. He wanted me to go back into art. He talked of sending our son to a good school. Jack grew up in Brooklyn, in a working class family. He yearned to spend more time with us both."

Miriam closed her eyes.

"All those dreams are gone now," she said quietly. "I'm going to stay here to see that Jack's killer gets the maximum penalty. Then I'm going to take our son away." Miriam looked up at Rochelle.

"You were born in Gloucester. I should go back home, too. Except where I grew up there was no sense of home. Maybe that's why Gloucester frightens me so much. It's all too real."

Terrence was back on the unit, testier than ever. As soon

as Rochelle came on duty Amanda called her over.

"Listen," she said. "Your boyfriend's back and he's gonna do what we say or he's outta here."

"Did he sign himself in voluntarily?"

"Yes, he did, Ms. Advocate."

"Then he has some say in his treatment," Rochelle answered.

"You bet your sweet ass he does."

Rochelle looked Amanda in the face.

"We're all mandated to treat the patients equitably. And we're required to treat each other professionally. I treat you that way and I expect the same treatment. If I don't get it, you can bet that I'll be filing a grievance."

Amanda's face reddened.

"A year on the unit and now you're running it."

"I'm not running anything," Rochelle persisted. "I know what the patients' rights are and I'm familiar with my own."

Turning, she walked away from Amanda.

"Just remember," Amanda shouted after her. "Your protector's gone. Things are different around here now."

Terrence was sitting by the window in his room.

"You should be in group," Rochelle said, entering.

"Tell me about it, sweetie."

Rochelle sat on the edge of his bed. The room was quiet. She watched the dust moats floating in a beam of sunlight. Terrence seemed thoughtful.

"What happened this time?" she asked.

Terrence sighed.

"I just can't cut it."

"Cut what?" Rochelle asked.
"Life!"
Rochelle shook her head.
"Do you think anybody can?"
"You seem to be able to."
"That's what you think," Rochelle said.
"It sure looks it."
"Looks can seem."
"Hey, that's good!"
"You like that?"
"I never knew you were so quick on the come back."
Rochelle laughed.
"Neither did I."
Terrence turned to face her.
"I like you a lot," he said.
"I like you, too."
"So let's get married."
"I'm already married."
"Don't you think I know that?"
Rochelle looked steadily at Terrence.
"I wish I could help you," she said.
"I'm beyond help."
"I don't believe anybody is beyond help."
"This baby is and he knows it."
"Then why do you keep coming back?"
Terrence gestured hopelessly with palms of his hands.
"It's an escape when things get to be too much."
"It can be a haven, too, a place of healing."
"The wounds are too deep," Terrence said flatly.
"Are you so sure?"

"Sure as shootin'," Terrence answered, turning again to look out the window.

That afternoon the entire staff of the hospital was summoned to a meeting. Rochelle heard the buzz of confused conversation as she walked down the corridor leading to the lecture room. Once she was there she found the administrative team and most of the doctors sitting in a half circle facing the nursing staff.

Dressed in a dark blue suit, the president dropped the bombshell.

"As of tomorrow this hospital will have merged with Beverly's under the umbrella of Northshore Health Care Systems." He pushed his white hair back over his ears.

There had been rumors during the year of merger offers and attempts, but no one expected this news. The nursing staff seemed stunned.

Rochelle walked slowly back to the unit. Behind her she could hear Amanda and Murray discussing something in lowered tones. She felt a heaviness come over her just as it had after she learned about Jack's death.

Terrence had finally agreed to go to group. Before she signed out for the day Rochelle went to his room to thank him for trying.

"Hey, this may be my last visit?"

"What do you mean?" Rochelle said.

"Didn't you hear? They're closing the unit."

"No one announced it at the meeting."

"Murray and Sue told us at group."

"At *group?*"

"Yup. The plan is to merge this unit with Beverly's."

There was an atmosphere of suspense in the unit, as if everyone were waiting for the other shoe to drop. Rochelle continued to see her patients. She gave out meds to a man with schizophrenia, she stopped to chat with a young mother suffering from postpartum depression. With Terrence, she made a special effort to support him as he attended group or, in Jack's absence, saw Murray one-on-one. The hospital's chief of psychiatry consulted with the staff, but no new psychiatrist was assigned to the unit.

Rochelle avoided Amanda, who went out of her way not to speak to Rochelle. And finally Rochelle received the notice she'd been expecting. As the newest member of the staff she had been laid off.

Sue came up to her on one of the last days.

"If it's any consolation I've been terminated, too," she said.

"Why you?"

"They've already got their complement of MSWs in Beverly."

"Won't there be more beds?" Rochelle asked.

"There won't. In fact, that unit's being downsized, too."

Rochelle was shocked.

"How can they downsize when they've just expanded their service area?"

"Apparently they can do anything they want," Sue said.

On her last day Rochelle started down the ward to say good-bye to Terrence.

"He's history," Amanda called out from behind the nurse's station.

"Has he been transferred to Beverly?"

"Signed himself out."

"Was he given the option?"

"What do you think, honey?"

Rochelle looked steadily at Amanda.

"The way decisions are being made around here I don't know what to think."

"Suit yourself," Amanda said, turning her back on Rochelle.

No one said good-bye to Rochelle and there was no one to thank her for her work or to wish her well. She picked up her paycheck on the last day and she walked out of the unit. Entering the empty elevator, she rode down to the lobby. When she went out through the automatic doors she knew so well from childhood, a terrible sense of disbelief came over her. She felt as if she were twelve years old again and had just heard the news of her father's death. She could remember every detail of having been let into the morgue to see Sonny's body—the marble slab, the pervasive odor of formaldehyde in the dark room, the sheet covering his body.

But she stopped the images there as though switching off a movie projector. She got into her car and drove home to meet her son.

Watching the 11 o'clock news that night, something she never did when she had to get up early for work, the announcement of a death in Gloucester penetrated her self-absorption. A Vietnam veteran had shot himself while playing Russian roulette.

Rochelle grabbed the remote control to punch up the

volume. As she did, she saw a photographic insert of Terrence's face in the upper left hand corner of the TV screen. Meanwhile, an emergency team in white was carrying a body on a stretcher down a flight of wooden steps. The sheet over the body seemed drenched in blood. Neighbors gathered on the sidewalk, staring as the body was loaded into an ambulance.

Rochelle rushed to the telephone. She called the ER, asking for her friend Ellen, who was the admissions nurse.

"He's dead," Ellen said. "I knew you'd call."

"Where is he now?"

"Downstairs. They're waiting for his family."

"Roberta's been notified?"

"The police are handling it."

"Where did it happen?" Rochelle asked.

"On Portagee Hill, in the apartment next to his. Apparently they were drinking at the kitchen table, Terrence and a couple of his army buddies. He challenged them to a game of Russian roulette. The police said one of them had an old Colt revolver. When the gun came around to Terrence, he put it up to his head and fired. Unfortunately, there was a bullet in the chamber. You still there?"

"I don't know what to say?"

"Whatever you do, Rochelle, don't blame yourself. He's been trying to kill himself for years."

"But he was beginning to open up," Rochelle pleaded. "He was going to group, doing his individual counseling. For the first time I felt there was hope. Then, bang, they close the unit on him. What kind of message is that for someone who's hanging by a thread?"

Ellen was quiet for a moment.

"Before they're done they'll be closing a lot more than one unit," she said angrily. "And they're gonna have a lot more blood than Terrence's on their hands. You can say you heard that from me."

Rochelle was sitting on the couch in the dark when Larry came home.

"I got the news on the radio," he said, sitting down next to Rochelle. "I'm so sorry."

Rochelle fell into Larry's arms.

"Just don't tell me not to blame myself," she sobbed.

Rochelle stood with Roberta and Terrence's daughter Charmayne as Terrence's coffin was lowered into a soldier's grave at Beechbrook Cemetery. The chaplain for the Veterans of Foreign Wars read the prayer. There was a gun salute by three uniformed veterans of Vietnam. A few of Terrence's friends came, their faces ravaged more by heroin and AIDS, Rochelle thought, than by any feeling of loss. There was no one from the unit. But Tony was there. He stood off to one side as the chaplain approached Roberta and Charmayne. When she saw him hand Roberta the folded flag from Terrence's coffin, Rochelle choked back her sobs.

Rochelle and Tony fell into step together as the scant number of mourners left the cemetery in the noon heat.

"We seem to meet at funerals," Tony said as they stood by Rochelle's car, parked with the others along the periphery of the cemetery.

"Was he a client?" Rochelle asked Tony.

"Terrence and I go back a long way." Tony shook his head disconsolately.

Rochelle noticed that he was getting bald. And there was a lot more gray in his mustache and beard.

"I'm just devastated," Tony said.

"There's so much to say." Rochelle felt herself hesitate. "Do you suppose we could talk sometime?"

Tony reached out and held her arm.

"Why don't we have lunch?"

"Is tomorrow too soon?"

"Tomorrow's fine. Want to meet at noon at McT's?"

Rochelle had known Tony as a teacher. And for the brief time she'd spent on welfare he'd been her caseworker. As she entered the restaurant she realized that their relationship was on a different level now. Meeting Tony for lunch felt like being on a date. Something about it thrilled Rochelle. And yet she felt a very deep need to speak with him about the events they'd shared. It was almost as if he held a key that would help her unlock their meaning for her.

Tony waved from a booth by the windows that looked out on the inner harbor. He looked handsome in a navy blue blazer and pink and white pinstriped shirt, which set off his dark red paisley tie. He had once told her that he'd learned how to dress in college, but as the son of a fisherman he still felt out of place

"Come, sit!" Tony held out his hand.

Once they'd ordered, Tony looked across the shiny table top at her.

"This is fun," he said. "I don't often take a real lunch."

"Neither do I," Rochelle said.

"We've two deaths to mourn," Tony began. "And I don't know where to start."

"How did you know Jack?" Rochelle asked.

"He'd call me from time to time about clients who needed food stamps or help with a disability application. When he found out that I taught literature part-time at the college, he wanted to talk about books. Jack majored in English at Harvard, you know."

Rochelle found herself smiling.

"That must have been fun."

"It was a challenge," Tony said. "There's little in any literature Jack wasn't familiar with."

"Where do you suppose he got the time for everything?"

Tony's eyes brightened.

"I had the feeling he never slept."

"He was tremendous with the patients at the unit."

"We talked about Terrence," Tony offered. "We talked about him a lot."

"I'm not surprised you knew Terrence."

Tony buttered his roll. Rochelle remembered how carefully trimmed he kept his nails. She saw wrinkles in the flesh of his hands that hadn't been there when she was his student.

"Terrence came to me in much the same way he came to you. He seemed always to be looking for something he couldn't quite articulate. I liked him a lot."

"Me, too," Rochelle said. "Only I couldn't seem to get through to him."

"That's two of us."

"Why is it that Jack's death has hit me so hard?"

Tony looked up from his salad.

"I think it's the shock of it. One minute you're working with someone, the next you hear they've been killed."

"I only had a couple of talks with him," Rochelle said. "But they were important to me."

Tony smiled as the waitress set their entrees down.

"Any talk with Jack was important. He was that kind of person. Not imposing, just simply all there for you—for himself as well."

Rochelle thought for a moment.

"How do you suppose people like Jack develop?"

"Jack would tell you that personhood is not innate, it's earned, struggled for."

"He must have worked hard to become himself."

"With Jack it all seemed so effortless. But you know, as a working class Jew at Harvard it wasn't easy. Oh, the academic work was. Jack could apply himself to anything. Still, he didn't think about psychiatry until late in his medical training. He was writing a lot. And then he met a teacher who was an analyst *and* a writer. That's all Jack needed. Suddenly he was on his way."

Rochelle hesitated before speaking.

"Where did he meet his wife?"

"At Harvard. She was doing graduate work in art history."

"Miriam's very warm."

"They seemed to have it all," Tony said. "And in a flash it was gone. Makes you wonder."

"There was Jack on top, and there was Terrence on the bottom."

"Think about Brucie," Tony said. "What if some Yuppie had been driving that pickup?"

Rochelle took a sip of her Diet Pepsi.

"This sounds like one of our classes."

"Jack and I talked like this a lot," Tony said. "I'm going to miss it."

Rochelle looked at her wristwatch.

"You probably have to get back to the office," she paused. "But I did want to talk a little about Terrence. I can't stop thinking about him."

"I'm not going to hurry," he said, taking another forkful of baked scrod. "They owe me a few lunch hours I never took."

Rochelle looked out at the lobster boats moored along the Town Landing dock. The sunlight sharpened their red and blue painted water lines. Above them on the pier, the metal traps were stacked, hundreds of them. Through the thick glass of the restaurant window she could hear the shrill cries of the gulls fighting over fragments of bait. This was what she loved about being home. It was what she had missed during her years in New Hampshire, the rawness of the waterfront, the rich smells of decaying fish.

"Look hard," Tony said. "One day it may all be gone. Once I couldn't get far enough away from fishing. Now all I can think about is saving it."

"It's our heritage," Rochelle said. "My father was a fisherman, so was Terrence . . . when they weren't drugging."

"What were you thinking about Terrence?"

"I wish I could have kept him alive," Rochelle said. "He didn't deserve to die."

"Yet he killed himself," Tony said. "Or he made a game out of doing it. I imagine he knew 'The Deer Hunter.' Being a Vietnam vet I'm sure he saw the film. But I also imagine it was more complicated than that. Growing up here you must have known his family."

"I knew *about* them," Rochelle said, folding her napkin.

"Living here, we've all got our histories," Tony said. "And most of us are familiar with each other's."

"Didn't you wish you could have helped Terrrence?"

"You bet I did," Tony replied. "But I've been a caseworker for a long time. Call it objectivity, or just call it callousness. I seemed to see it all unfolding as from a distance. I won't say I predicted its outcome. But I figured that one way or another Terrence would do himself in. There was just too much against him. Too much of that history. We both know it wasn't just Vietnam. Vietnam might never have happened to him. Look at the junkies who didn't go to war. They're still trying to die, one way or another."

Rochelle found herself looking Tony in the face.

"What is it about this town? Why are there so many people punishing themselves? Why, when they needed the psych unit so badly, did they close it? What's wrong with the hospital?"

"Let's shift the question," Tony said. "What's wrong with the culture? What kind of society do we live in that lets its young people drug themselves into oblivion? And what about their parents—their grandparents? If it isn't drugs it's alcohol. And those are only symptoms!"

"Are you trying to say that we're up against too much?" Rochelle asked.

"When I first became a social worker, I believed that with an understanding of human behavior and a little good will you could do some good in the world."

"And now what do you believe?"

"Would you be surprised if I told you I don't believe in anything?"

"Nothing at all?"

"I suppose I find some sense of meaning in the tragic. We come into this world by accident, we grope our way toward death. We learn by suffering, or we don't. But we still die."

"I'm not ready for that," Rochelle said. "I can't handle the starkness."

"What does Freud say about us?"

"He says that our instincts are murderous and what saves us is not God or religion but ruthlessly pursued self-examination."

"And not everyone is vouchsafed self-knowledge."

"Not everyone," Rochelle said. "But you know, at some level Terrence had it."

"I agree. Terrence and I talked a lot. He knew himself better than most people."

"But he still killed himself."

"So did Primo Levi, and there were few people as self-aware as Levi, or who'd suffered as much."

"Are you implying that self-awareness isn't any guarantee?"

Tony looked across the table at her.

"There are no rewards for good behavior. That's what I'm saying."

Rochelle just shook her head.

"Tony?" she asked. "I know how well you teach. Why didn't you stay at the university? What made you come back here?"

"That's a whole other story. Maybe sometime I'll share it with you."

Rochelle reached for the check, but Tony beat her to it.

"This is on me," he said.

"I feel we've just started talking," Rochelle said. "Can we do this again? Would you like to have supper some night with Larry and me?"

"I'd love to. Just give me a buzz."

At home that night Rochelle told Larry about her lunch with Tony.

"We talked about a lot of things," she said. "But I came away with my question unanswered. I still can't figure out why I'm so preoccupied with Terrence."

"Ask yourself this," Larry said. "Sonny and Terrence. Weren't they the same age? And didn't they look a lot alike. I mean growing up, they each had that Frank Zappa mustache and long hair. They boxed, they fished. They were into dope early. Terrence goes to Vietnam. Sonny's number never comes up in the draft lottery. But they both end up in the same place, hustling for a fix."

"Oh, my God!" Rochelle said.

"What I'm suggesting," Larry continued. "What seems to me is that Terrence turned into Sonny for you. He was your dad all over again. Only this time you thought you could save him. It was like bringing Sonny back from the dead. You got obsessive about it."

"I knew it, I just knew it!" Rochelle spoke excitedly. "I became overinvolved. Jack was warning me."

"You weren't talking about Terrence, but I knew you were thinking about him all the time."

"It must have made you angry."

"I can't say it didn't." Larry said.

"And what about the kids? Wasn't I paying attention to them?"

"I don't think little Larry noticed. He's so tied up with his friends. But Tiffany came to me one night when you were working. She was worried. Remember, she's been through your depressions with you."

Rochelle sighed.

"The poor kid. I've got to tell her what's been happening."

"She'll understand." Larry said. "It's going to be hard with Tiffany in college next year. It'll be like losing a daughter."

Rochelle took Larry's face in her hands.

"Just think I had a whole staff of professionals around me, but the answer was right here. My own husband turns out to be the best shrink!"

"Hey, I've been living with you all these years!"

Rochelle hugged Larry.

"Maybe getting laid off was good for me. Maybe I need some time to reflect on what's happened."

"Why don't you just sit tight for a while and collect your unemployment."

Rochelle sat up.

"I couldn't do that! It would feel like being back on welfare."

"You didn't let me finish," Larry broke in. "I didn't say do nothing. You've been talking for years about getting your master's. There's a part-time program at BC School of Social Work. I saw it advertised the other day in the Globe. In fact, I cut it out of the education section for you."

"Larry, what can I say?"

"Let me go get it for you. You can tell me what you think."

"I think it sounds great," Rochelle said. "I could probably go to class days while little Larry's in school. Maybe I could pay for it by working part time."

"Have you checked our savings account lately?"

"But I can't always be the taker."

"Someday I may need it," Larry said smiling. "Right now there's enough for you. And there's some for Tiffany too."

The next morning after Larry had left for work and the school bus had picked Tiffany up, Rochelle stood at the front door watching little Larry running across the street to meet his friends. Once she picked up around the house, something she'd only been able to do on weekends when she was working, she got on the telephone to the admissions office at Boston College. She asked for a set of applications and she made an appointment to meet with the Dean of the Graduate School of Social Work. She also called Simmons College and Boston University, requesting information on their social work programs. Nursing had been rewarding, if difficult, she decided. Maybe being a clinical social worker would give her a different kind of challenge. She would have to see. Meanwhile, she busied herself in the basement, making a place to study in the corner, where she'd built some shelves for her textbooks and where there was an old, oak-topped desk.

When the mail came later that morning, she found a package in her delivery box. Right away she noticed it was from Jack's wife. She opened the outer wrapping to discover a note from Miriam: "This was one of Jack's favorite books. I thought you might like to have it to remember him by. Thanks for coming to visit me."

Rochelle tore open the package. It contained the collected poems of Wallace Stevens in one large volume. The dust jacket was a rubbed and faded blue with Stevens' portrait on it.

"I can't believe it," Rochelle said to herself, as she sat down and began turning pages covered with notes in what must have been Jack's minute handwriting. The first poem she came to was "The Snow Man."

Broken Trip

After lunch with Rochelle, Tony returned to his office to find a client in the waiting room. He was a wiry little man, white-haired and ramrod stiff. When Tony looked him up in the Central Data Base, he couldn't find his name.

"Never been here," said Walter Brown. "Guess I never had to."

Brown explained that he was facing eviction from the apartment he'd occupied for more than thirty years.

"Lost my wife," he said, "and my landlord sold the house. New one doubled the rent. Without her Social Security check I can't hack it. Someone said I'd better come down here and see what you could do for me."

Tony sat back in his chair. As Brown told him how much income he had and what the new rent was, Tony ran through the options in his mind.

"We could do a little income maximization," he offered. "You'd probably qualify for food stamps and I could send you over to Fuel Assistance. The stamps would reduce your monthly grocery bill, while the fuel assistance might cover a portion of your winter's gas or oil bill, depending upon what you heat with. That would take some of the rent pressure off."

Brown seemed attentive, so Tony continued.

"Are you disabled in any way?"

Brown shook his head.

"I've always been fit as a fiddle."

"That rules out SSI," Tony said. "Are you a veteran?"

Brown sat up straighter in his chair.

"World War Two combat vet. European theater. Battle of the Bulge."

"That's good," Tony said. "You'd have a service related priority if you applied for elderly housing. Have you considered that?"

"I'd hoped to avoid it," Brown said, his eyes narrowing to a squint.

"You may not have a choice," Tony said. "If you were only paying thirty percent of your total income for rent your financial troubles would be over."

"I never thought about it that way."

"How *did* you think about it?" Tony heard an edge of impatience creeping into his voice.

"I always thought of old folks' housing as welfare."

"Try looking at it another way," Tony offered. "You've worked all your life. Your taxes helped build the kind of housing that makes life a little easier for the elderly. Especially those like you who are alone."

Brown appeared to agree.

"Say, I didn't get your name."

"Tony Russo."

"Your old man fish?"

"He owned the Santa Clara."

"Gillnetter! I knew him. Used to take out at Gorton's in the old days."

As Brown became more voluble, Tony wondered where he'd seen him before. It was his flinty eyes that seemed familiar, along with the physicality of the man, the tension his body held.

"That was my father."

"He's dead, isn't he? By Jesus, they're all dead, all them old Guineas." Brown paused. "Hey, don't get me wrong, I'm a Nova Scotia herring choker myself!"

Tony smiled. "We're all from someplace else."

"That says it. Now you was telling me about the housing?"

"I could send you to the Housing Authority. As a combat veteran, who's probably paying more than fifty percent of his income in rent, you'd get top priority."

"I would?" Brown seemed excited.

"I suspect they'd offer you an apartment in less than six months."

"That soon?"

Tony felt like saying, "We aim to please." But he decided that it would be unprofessional. At any rate, he liked this Brown.

"Let's do the food stamp application now," he said. "Then I'll send you over to Fuel Assistance. After you've applied there, you can walk over to the Housing Authority and sign-up for housing. Is that too much?"

"Time's what I got on my hands since I lost the wife."

After Walter Brown left, Tony had hoped for a minute to reflect on what he and Rochelle discussed over lunch. He was afraid his old student might think he was becoming too cynical. Instead, he took a call from the director of the homeless shelter, who wanted to talk about a young woman who'd recently become a guest.

"What can I help with?" Tony asked Jill.

"I thought she might be eligible for General Relief."

"I take it she can't work," Tony said.

"She can't do much of anything."

"What if I talked to her about housing. Maybe we could get her into a single room somewhere. Once she's in, we could go for benefits to stabilize her."

"It's worth a try," Jill said.

"What's her name?"

"Anouk," Jill said. "Good luck."

When he heard the name Tony immediately guessed who the woman was. He'd run into her one day during lunch at the Glass Sailboat on Duncan Street. The clerks appeared to be giving her food. Wondering where she'd come from, Tony watched her staring endlessly at the shelves of vitamins and herbal remedies. As warm as the weather was, she was wearing an expensive Norwegian sweater and Alpine boots, her long brown hair combed out straight.

Anouk had skin that was transparently pale, with Slavic eyes set in a wide face. Tony found her standing by herself as though attending to inner voices. But she didn't have the disheveled look or the slightly stale body odor one often associates with a deinstitutionalized patient. She seemed to take particular care of her appearance. As she moved about the café, her skin gave off the fragrance of patchouli oil. Once she began to speak with people at the communal tables, Anouk became suddenly articulate. Her face brightened.

When Jill sent her up from the shelter the next morning,

Tony didn't think Anouk recognized him from the café. Neither did she seem enthusiastic when he offered to help her fill out the application for public assistance. After he'd completed the initial intake, he knew little more about this woman than he'd learned from Jill. She said she'd grown up in Gloucester and had been sent away to school. Otherwise, she was vague about her subsequent activities. Still, he felt edgy with Anouk, as if she was a new student and he was afraid of not making a good impression. After she left, the fragrance of patchouli persisted in the office. Tony found himself thinking about her more than he usually thought about a case.

Before he straightened up his desk to leave for the day, Tony was handed a memo by the director's secretary. A staff meeting had been scheduled for ten the next morning with the Regional Director. No sooner had the memo been distributed than the speculations began. Cheri, the receptionist, came over to the cubicle next to Tony's office where Nancy the E&T coordinator worked.

"The shit's hitting the fan," Cheri said.

"You mean they're gonna do it?" Nancy asked.

Tony knew immediately what they were talking about. For months there'd been rumors that as part of the governor's new Welfare Reform package they were going to consolidate services. This meant shutting down some of the field offices. Gloucester's was long expected to be one of them. If that happened, the clients would be shunted over to Salem.

"It doesn't matter that we've got one of the largest caseloads in the Commonwealth?" Tony had argued with his director when the rumors first surfaced. "Or that the recipients don't have transportation?"

"Nothing matters but the perception that the taxpayers' money is being saved," said Chuck, who was not sympathetic to Welfare Reform.

As he walked home along Prospect Street, the air mild and the sky darkening to purple, Tony anticipated what would be announced at the meeting. The prospect of change after so many years of stability ought to have disturbed him. Instead, he found himself thinking about Anouk. The shelter would have just opened and he wondered if she'd be there yet. Part of him wanted to continue down Prospect to Main Street instead of turning up Mt. Vernon, where he lived. He pictured himself stopping in at the shelter to have a chat with Jill with whom he'd worked for years. But he knew he would really be entering the shelter to see Anouk.

Next day's meeting went as expected. Consolidation was becoming a litany in social services just as it had taken hold in the corporate world. Several hospitals on the North Shore had merged. So had a number of area mental health and elder services agencies. Now it was the turn of the Welfare Department.

The Regional Director was pleasant enough about it.

"These are the facts," he explained. "After the new legislation with its mandatory work requirement goes into effect, we expect substantial drops in the number of families on AFDC. We'll be centralizing services to create one-stop-shopping centers. In these offices we'll do intake and assessment and we'll handle all the Employment and Training and child care requests."

Tony was about to ask what would happen to those families who would be summarily terminated when the proposed two-year time limit on benefits went into effect, those who'd probably become destitute or homeless once they lost the minimal income floor that welfare provided. Wouldn't caring for them create new demands? Besides, what was the Department *really* doing to provide well-paying jobs or to train those recipients who lacked skills?

But he knew it was useless. The directors didn't make policy. Policy was being crafted by the governor and his supporters in the legislature with the help of consultants from states like California, which had already retooled their public benefits systems, states that had begun effectively to drive poor people out.

In answer to a question from one of the workers about the fate of their jobs, the Regional Director said it was too early to say.

"You'll all be given a chance to transfer. There'll be some buyout options, too. That's about all I can tell you at the moment."

The Regional Director gathered up his papers to leave.

"Incidentally," he added, turning once more to the staff. "The department is changing its name. In keeping with our new mission to end public welfare as a way of life, we'll now be called the Department of Transitional Assistance."

Back at his desk, Tony stared out the window at the harbor. Silhouetted on the horizon was the skyline of Boston. It was a view he'd come to prize each day, one he'd surely miss. The prospect of commuting to work didn't excite him, either. What would he be looking at if they transferred him to Salem, or Quincy even?

When the receptionist buzzed him asking if he'd see Anouk without an appointment, his first reaction was to refuse. She'd have to learn to respect protocol, he decided. But that decision conflicted with a concern that she might be in trouble, so he asked Cheri to send her in.

"Last time you mentioned housing," Anouk began haltingly. "Where I stay is important because I'm sensitive to certain chemicals. Smoking bothers me, too."

"How are you dealing with that in the shelter," Tony asked.

"If I can't breathe I leave."

"Where do you go then?"

Anouk looked down.

"I sleep in the woods."

"Even when it's cold?"

She nodded.

A few days later Tony saw Anouk standing on the corner of Middle and Pleasant streets, near the center of town. Facing her was a man with a red plaid tam on his head. He seemed to be trying to communicate with her. It was nearly 6 p.m. and the light of the setting sun imparted a bronze-like glow to the red brick buildings up and down the street. As soon as Tony recognized Anouk he slowed down.

She stood impassively. As Tony approached the couple, he could hear the man's voice, coaxing Anouk into going somewhere with him. He held his face close to hers. It was as if he were trying to reason with a child. He sounded drunk. Expecting that Anouk would notice him, perhaps even call out from across the street where he stood, Tony stopped. But she stood the way she did in the Glass Sailboat, with a blank look in her eyes. Tony had a sense that she was there in body only. Hearing the man's voice get louder and watching his hands flailing at his sides, Tony started to cross the street towards the couple. Then he restrained himself. He went on walking the length of the block. When he turned to cross the street again, he saw the man still gesturing. Anouk was as immobile as a statue.

"I guess there's nothing I could really do," he told Jill, as he described the situation to her on the phone the next day.

"If she didn't ask for help you couldn't possibly intervene."

"What if he hurt her?"

"Anouk was in the shelter last night," Jill said. "But she did seem more distracted than usual."

She paused.

"You're frustrated, aren't you?"

"I'm used to working with people who tell you what they want."

"Maybe Anouk is telling us what she *doesn't* need," Jill said.

A week later Anouk stopped going to the shelter.

"At first we thought she'd just wandered away," Jill reported. "Then one night Anouk came by for her things. She told me she was staying in an apartment not far from the shelter."

When Jill named the principal tenant, Tony recognized one of his own clients, a man who suffered from a bipolar disorder. But he wasn't the person Tony had seen Anouk with on the street corner.

Shortly afterward, Jill reported that she'd gone to visit

Anouk, but she couldn't get in.

"She's placed duct tape around the door between her room and the rest of the apartment," Jill said. "And it looks like she's getting in and out of the room through the window."

One afternoon a woman introducing herself as Anouk's mother appeared at his office.

"I came to thank you for helping my daughter," she said.

Youthful and stunningly dressed, Christiana had the same broad face as her daughter, but her hair was ash blond, her fingernails painted a deep red.

"We're trying," Tony said.

"Take my word for it, it's not easy."

Disregarding the NO SMOKING sign, Christiana lit a cigarette.

"Could she live with you?"

"That and anything else," Christiana replied.

"Is this typical?" Tony asked. "The way she seems to move around a lot."

"Anouk's done it ever since she was an adolescent. But I'm intrigued by the way she's gravitated back to where she grew up."

Christiana looked about for an ashtray. When she didn't find one, she flicked the ashes from her unfiltered cigarette onto the office floor.

"As a child Anouk was always introverted," she continued. "During puberty she became quite odd. Her father and I were separating. Once we'd sold the house here and moved to Connecticut, we placed her in a boarding school. She drew and painted constantly. After her father died, she began having these episodes. She spent a couple of years in and out of hospitals. Then she seemed well enough to go to art school, but that didn't last."

"What about the chemical sensitivities she claims to have?"

Christiana gestured with the upraised palms of her hands.

"The psychiatrists say it's her response to a world she finds hostile."

Drawing reflectively on her cigarette, Christiana confided to Tony that Anouk's father had committed suicide. He was a painter, born in Budapest. They'd met in Paris as students. He named Anouk after the actress Anouk Aimee. "Perhaps you remember her from *La Dolce Vita*."

"Did Anouk love her father?" Tony asked.

"She idolized him. But Sandor never forgave himself for her illness."

Christiana's deeply tanned face masked whatever anguish she may have felt. Tony noticed that her nose was more finely modeled than her daughter's, the corners of her mouth slightly creased.

"Jill and I would like to help," he said. "I've offered housing to Anouk since she seems to feel comfortable here in town. It would be safer than where she's staying now." Tony tried to choose his words carefully.

"Of course," her mother said. "It's better if I know where she is."

Looking around for a place to dispose of her cigarette, Christiana cleared her throat. Tony pushed his gray metal wastebasket toward her. She removed a note pad and gold-plated pencil from her soft leather shoulder bag. Jotting an address and telephone number on the pad, she handed Tony the single slip of paper.

"Feel free to call me," she said. Then she smiled at Tony.

"You don't remember me, do you? I sat in front of you in senior English."

"Chris Wuorinen?"

"That's me."

"You wore a coat," Tony said. "An extraordinary fur coat. I remember it because no one at Gloucester High School ever had on such a coat."

"It was my mother's mink," Christiana said. "The winter I wore it was the winter she died. That's when I got kicked out of Farmington. As punishment my father kept me home for a semester. But I didn't think of it as being so grim. I loved it. You kids were having a blast!"

Tony laughed, recalling the beautiful blond transfer student who'd suddenly appeared in Miss Harris's honors class wearing a Black Watch plaid kilt and tan cashmere sweater. She seemed so different from the other girls, so distant and unattainable.

"You know I had a terrible crush on you," Christiana said. "Do you remember those nights I'd call you about the homework? I understood perfectly well what the assignments were. I just wanted to hear your voice, to have you to myself after class. I knew you had a girl friend, but I still liked you. You were so different from the prep school boys I'd dated, so smart without being stuck up. I thought it was fabulous that you were Italian. I couldn't believe your father was a fishing captain!"

After Christiana had left, Tony noticed that the office

smelled faintly of her perfume, a fragrance that seemed suddenly chilling.

Just then Walter Brown called to report that he was number three on the waiting list for elderly housing.

"Fuel Assistance cleared up my heating bill," he said. "And the food stamps are helping. I never thought I'd have to resort to them."

"Whatever works," Tony said. "And keep me posted on the housing."

Replacing the receiver, he wondered if he'd ever seen Brown before his first visit. The steely blue eyes, the way they appeared almost to be hooded by paper-thin lids. Maybe he was just imagining some resemblance. After twenty-five years in human services he'd seen a lot of people. Not to speak of those like Chris Wuorenin who emerged from his past!

As soon as a room in a women's residential facility became available that summer, Tony asked Jill if she could find Anouk and tell her about it.

"She was very ambivalent," Jill reported back. "I don't think she wants to be around other people. You know, she's sleeping on the beach again."

"What happened to the shared living?"

"Your guess is as good as mine," Jill said.

When Tony ran into Anouk at lunch one day, she barely acknowledged his greeting. She was wearing a pair of gray shorts and her hair was matted. Around her neck she'd tied a green cotton sweater. Tony noticed that her ankles were caked with dirt, her legs dark from exposure to the sun.

That night after work he decided to walk over to Stage

Fort Park, near the beach where Jill thought Anouk had been hiding. As he walked along the Boulevard, he felt foolish among the evening joggers. What business was it of his that a client might be sleeping at Half Moon Beach? Of course, it was against the law to stay on the beaches after dark, but let the police find her. They were familiar with Anouk. They might even convince her to return to the shelter where she'd at least be safe.

Tony wandered over the entire park, checking the beach and the wooded pathways above it. Then he stood for a time watching a Little League game. He even visited the public toilets. As the light fell, he returned to the beach. He was hungry, his vision blurred. Once it was dark, he turned back toward town, stopping at Valentino's for pizza and a glass of wine.

Sitting in the restaurant window that looked out on Main Street, Tony kept imagining that he saw Anouk in the faces of passersby. As he sipped his Chianti, he thought himself into Anouk's state of mind. What would she think? Would she see herself reflected in the dark glass against a backdrop of unlighted storefronts?

Heading homeward, Tony passed The Rigger, a fishermen's bar located just a block up the street from the pizza parlor. On impulse he looked in through one of its fake porthole windows. In the dim light he saw a group of men sitting at the bar. They were watching a ball game on the overhead TV. Directly underneath the big console, in the glow of the monitor's screen, he recognized Anouk. His breath came up short as he saw her face, blue in the light cast by the monitor. From the rapt look in her eyes she appeared to be giving her full attention to a conversation. But as he stood staring through the dirty pane of the circular window, Tony noticed that no one was speaking to her.

The following night he went looking again for Anouk, and several nights afterward. When he couldn't find her, Tony thought he should go to the police and report her missing. Then it occurred to him that the police might find it odd that he was searching for a client in the middle of the night. Finally, he went home. But he carried with him a feeling of uneasiness and foreboding that followed him into a fitful sleep.

The next morning Jill was waiting for Tony at his office. As he signed in with shaking hands, she told him that the police had called her at 7 a.m. A neighbor walking his dog had found Anouk lying unconscious at the edge of the park.

"She was bleeding from the ears," Jill said.

Immediately they called Christiana. Then Tony and Jill drove to the hospital to wait for her outside the Intensive Care Unit. The doctor in charge told them that Anouk had a fractured skull. A police inspector, who was waiting to question them, said that she'd been assaulted with a fist-sized rock. They found the weapon on the ground next to her. She also appeared to have been raped.

As soon as Christiana arrived, the doctor conducted her into the room where Anouk was receiving treatment.

"Thank God she's not in a coma," she told Tony and Jill when she emerged.

Then Tony and Jill were allowed to enter the room where Anouk lay under an oxygen tent. Her face was so swollen and bruised Tony could scarcely recognize her. It looked as though they had shaved most of her head. She was motionless, her lips blue, eyes closed. Tony could only hear the sound of the breathing apparatus.

When he left the hospital, he went to the police station to report Anouk's confrontation with the man in the red plaid tam. He also said that Anouk had lived for a time with a client of his, who was mentally ill and known to be violent. He returned to his office, but he could do no work. Then Jill called to report that Christiana was having Anouk transferred to a hospital in New Haven.

The next morning Tony's boss invited him into his office.

"We're ceasing operations here on September 1," Chuck told Tony. "You've got two choices. You can transfer to Quincy or you can take the buyout package."

"What about Salem?" Tony asked.

"No more openings. Remember, the entire Beverly office has to be placed."

Chuck was a portly man with long, gray hair and a goatee. He and Tony had always worked well together, and Tony knew that Chuck would be retiring when they shut down. He also knew that Chuck would do whatever he could to help him.

"What do you suggest?" Tony asked.

"Go for the buyout," Chuck said. "You've got a good twenty-five years in. You'll get full pension along with a year's severance. It's pretty sweet. If you continue to teach you'll be rolling in clover."

"What if I don't want to?"

"Hey," Chuck said. "Whoever asked for a golden handshake?"

The police couldn't locate Anouk's assailant. They told

Tony that his bipolar client and the man with the red tam appeared to have alibis. Detectives assumed that Anouk might have been followed after leaving The Rigger. It was also possible she'd been surprised by one of the nighttime inhabitants of the park, someone who'd been aware of her habits and was stalking her.

In mid-August, Christiana called to report that Anouk had been moved from the New Haven hospital to a private psychiatric facility. At first she'd been deeply withdrawn, in a near catatonic state. But now Anouk seemed to be regaining her composure. Soon she would be discharged in her mother's care.

Tony closed his cases, laboring over the intricate paperwork he'd gotten accustomed to after so many years in the Welfare Department. Most of the staff knew where they'd be relocated and there was the usual grumbling. Now that his termination, his forced retirement, was nearly upon him, Tony realized that he'd done nothing to prepare for the change in his life. He was scheduled to begin teaching his usual evening course at the college after Labor Day. But what would become of his days? Should he apply to teach full-time? Or should he look for new work? At fifty-five he was too young to retire. Yet Chuck had done it. He'd done it apparently without looking backward once. Could Tony do the same thing?

And what had it all been about? he wondered. One minute he and Donna had been comfortably settled in Madison, his wife working as a computer programmer while Tony completed courses toward the doctorate in English. He'd been awarded an assistantship, he loved the teaching. The university was an exciting place to be during the Vietnam years. They went to demonstrations against the war, and after the peace marches they went to parties where the talk was energizing. Students and teachers mingled equitably, and the ideas they exchanged, the dialogue they engaged in, seemed as vital as the people around them. It was what Tony had lived for his entire life.

But conflicts emerged. Donna wanted children; she missed her family. She complained about being homesick for Gloucester.

"Please! Let's go home, Tony," she'd insist. "This place gives me the creeps."

"You promised to stick it out with me. I'm just starting to get a handle on my life."

"Can't you do that in Gloucester?"

"Not when I've got a good shot at a job in Berkeley."

Donna would invariably break down:

"I can't take it any more! I gotta have a normal life!"

That was when the ultimatums began. Donna was on the phone a lot with her parents. They wanted to know what was wrong with Tony. Why couldn't he come home where he and Donna belonged? Tony could find a teaching job nearby, they insisted. And wasn't it time for them to start a family?

Donna's family pressured Tony's. So Tony began to hear from his mother.

"What kind of son are you never coming home to see your parents?" she'd demand. "Why are you being so selfish? Think of your wife. She needs to be near her mother. And when you gonna act like a man? Them books ain't gonna make you no baby!"

Reluctantly, Tony agreed to come home. Without his doctorate he couldn't get a tenure-track appointment, so he started teaching part-time at the community college. When an opening was advertised for a caseworker at the local Welfare office, he took the State Civil Service exam and got the job. The department paid to send him to social work school at BU, where he took courses in case work, counseling and social policy. At first the job was dull, the paperwork overwhelming. But as soon as he began to work with families on AFDC, he felt he'd discovered something as stimulating as teaching. He loved helping people to solve the problems of their lives. And he found that working with Gloucester residents brought him back into the heart of the community. He began to understand the soul of the place he thought he'd abandoned forever. The only problems he couldn't solve were his own.

Once Donna was back home, she and her cousin Ginny began seeing a lot of each other. Whenever Tony asked his wife if she wanted to go out for supper, it was always, "Naw, Ginny 'n me got plans."

Spending more and more time with Ginny, Donna seemed to have lost interest in starting a family. She cut her hair short and wore pants. The two women would drive to the Mall once a week or go bowling together. Sometimes they took in a movie, while Busty worked overtime and Tony taught classes at the college. Ginny and her husband Busty didn't have kids either. Considering that, family members figured Donna and Ginny were probably good for each other.

Tony and Donna hardly ever made love; and if he moved to initiate sex, Donna would pull away.

"What's wrong?" Tony would whisper in the uneasy darkness.

"Nothing, I'm tired."

"I'm worried about us. We never used to be this way."

"I don't wanna talk. I got work tomorrow."

Each night they came home from work to strained silences. Donna took the second bedroom, leaving Tony by himself in their marriage bed. Talk continued at a minimum, until Tony told Donna that they should see a marriage counselor.

"Do what you want," she said on her way out to the movies with Ginny.

A day later Tony came home to find all of Donna's clothing gone. Next thing he knew Busty was on the phone.

"Where's Ginny? Her closet's empty!"

"Donna's is too."

"I can't find her car either!" Busty screamed through the receiver.

With his father now dead and his mother in a nursing home, Tony's parents were spared the scandal and embarrassment, the *vergogna* that every Italian family dreaded. But Busty always thought it had hastened his father's death.

"*Nun' ti dimentica!*" Big Busty shook his finger at his son. "A good Italian girl would never do such a thing."

Donna and Ginny had eloped to Florida. Divorce followed, and then the sale of the house.

When Tony moved his books and papers into his new apartment on Mt. Vernon Street, with its clean white walls and panoramic view of the waterfront, he felt as if he were starting all over again. He would work and teach. The rest of the time would be his to study and read. There had always been a monkish side to him, an asceticism he yearned after, even as a lapsed Catholic. Henceforth, he embraced that part of himself.

Shortly before noon he received a call from Christiana. Anouk had left the house one morning and hadn't returned.

"The police can't find her. No one has seen her. I'm beside myself!"

"I'll alert Jill," Tony said. "You may have heard, the state is closing this office."

"But what will people do? Where will they go for help? Where will *you* be?"

"I don't know," Tony answered. "I wish I did."

Tony's last client was Walter Brown, who came though the door of the empty office smiling.

"Just dropped by to thank you in person," he said, sitting familiarly across from Tony. "They've offered me an apartment in the new high rise. Hey, it's only a couple streets over from where I live!"

"That's great news," Tony said.

"I owe it all to you."

"You did the leg work, Mr. Brown."

"Brownie. Say, I think I know you. Didn't you used to work at the Seafood Center?"

"I did," Tony said. "The summer after I graduated from high school."

"I thought I remembered your name," Brownie said. "You used to eat with us on the loading platform. You, me, Gus. Remember Manuel, the Portagee?"

"Whatever happened to him?" Tony asked, as that distant summer slowly returned to him.

"He retired. Him and his old lady went back to the old country."

"Gus died, right?"

"Yeah, that same summer," Brownie said.

"There was another guy," Tony recalled. "He was missing a finger."

"That was George. He lost it in a band saw accident."

"What became of George?" Tony asked.

"Killed himself. Poor bastard jumped overboard in front of his house in Magnolia. Nobody knew why."

"You worked for Gorton's a long time," Tony said.

"Over forty years. Can you beat that? Slave all your life and you end up begging for a place to live. That ain't what we fought the war for."

"No, it isn't," Tony agreed.

"But that's all water over the dam," Brownie said, getting up. "I really come to thank you."

Tony stood up, too.

"I appreciate your visit." Tony shook his hand.

At the door Brownie turned. Those oddly remembered blue eyes sought his face.

"I seem to remember you was going to be a doctor. What happened?"

"It was just a pipedream," Tony laughed. "Once I got to college I realized I didn't have it in me to study medicine."

"But you're still taking care of people," Brownie said.

After Cheri shut the switchboard down, Tony was the last person to leave. Chuck had said his good-byes earlier in the day, the others were on vacation before starting their new jobs. As he took one final lingering look out his office window at the tranquil harbor, he thought of Anouk who'd predictably vanished again. He recalled her wide face and those astonishing dark eyes, which she must have inherited from her father. What had she evoked in him that sent him searching for her in the night? Was Anouk the elusive wife, some part of himself he could not get hold of? Or was she the daughter he never had? Tony wondered as he pictured again the people he'd met in his office and soon lost, people whose lives had briefly touched his and then faded like the fragrance of Anouk's hair.

He took his favorite way home, along the waterfront. Keeping the Fitz Hugh Lane house to his left, he passed the Building Center, at whose wharves the city's coal and lumber had once been unloaded. On his right was the Gloucester Marine Railways whose existence was endangered now that the fishing fleet had been diminished. He'd worked there one summer, too, and at the company's other shipyard on Rocky Neck, caulking and painting boats. Growing up, he'd put in time at just about every fish plant and marine facility on the waterfront.

Leaving Harbor Loop, he passed Gorton's abandoned cannery where he'd once packed cod fish cakes. Below that facility, on the old flake wharf, were the pen rooms where he'd shoveled the bones and entrails of red fish that were converted into mink food. He'd even loaded hundred pound bags of the once popular by-product onto boxcars at the Boston & Maine railroad, in a freight yard that no longer existed. Approaching the Seafood Center, he saw the loading platform that Brownie had mentioned. Covered now by a facade of tinted glass and fitted out with double doors, the scene of their dinners and mugups had been converted into an atrium, a fancy new entrance to the old plant. Even the workers' cars in the parking lot were more expensive now.

Gloucester was changing, and not for the better. Yet something had drawn him back here, away from the glamour of the university, the dream of eventually teaching at Berkeley. It was something that lay far deeper than what he'd believed was his acquiescence to a homesick wife. For Tony had needed to return as much if not more than Donna had, Donna who'd escaped as soon as she could.

Tony had remained. He'd stayed put even after Donna had run away, when there was no longer the need to stay. He'd stayed and taught the children of the very people he'd worked with on the waterfront; and he'd stayed to help the ones who needed more than school to feel better about themselves. He didn't know if he'd succeeded; he'd certainly failed with Anouk.

I guess it's been a broken trip, he thought, remembering what his father used to say when the long haul to the fishing grounds had seemed a bust—and now the industry itself had "come a broker." Nevertheless, as Tony left the Seafood Center behind and started homeward in the fading September light, up Prospect Street toward the blue cupolas of the church of Our Lady of Good Voyage, he knew that he had made the right choice, just as his father had, going back to the sea again and again.

✧

About the Author

Peter Anastas was born in the city he writes about. For thirty years he worked in the heart of the community, at Action, Inc., Gloucester's anti-poverty agency, where he was Director of Advocacy & Housing. His previous publications include *Glooskap's Children: Encounters with the Penobscot Indians of Maine* (Beacon Press) and *At the Cut*, a memoir of growing up in Gloucester in the 1940s, along with fiction and non-fiction in *Niobe, The Falmouth Review, Stations, America One, The Larcom Review, Polis, Split Shift, the Café Review,* and *Sulfur.*

GLAD DAY PUBLISHING COLLABORATIVE
(After an engraving by William Blake)

Book publishing is now in the hands of a few media conglomerates whose concern is not books, certainly not with literature or social change. With the elimination of independent bookstores and distribution through the chains the promotional lifetime of a book may now be measured in weeks.

Our particular purpose is to bridge the gap between imaginative literature and political articles and criticism which have been fixed under the labels of "Fiction" and "Non-Fiction." But the split has diminished literature and its usefulness to society. With these constraints writers find themselves engaged in self-censorship that has to do both with artistic and formal considerations and with what can be said. The hope of a literature that is positively useful has inspired us to call our publishing imprint GLAD DAY.

Other books published by GLAD DAY COLLABORATIVE:

History and Spirit by Joel Kovel
   An enquiry into the philosophy of liberation.

Serious Kissing by Bárbara Selfridge
   Stories

Travels in Altai by Robert Nichols
   Stories

Girl in Movement by Eva Kollisch
   A memoir

Teacha! by Gerry Albarelli
   Stories from a yeshiva

Ecological Investigations: The Web and the Wheel
   by Roy Morrison
   Speculative essays

A Voyage to New Orleans by Elisé Reclus
   Translated and edited by John Clark and Camille Martin
   An anarchist's impressions of the Old South.

Swords that Shall Not Strike: Poems of Protest and Rebellion
   by Kenneth Rexroth
   Edited, with an introductory essay, by Geoffrey Gardner

Big Bust at Tyrone's Rooming House by James Gallant
   A novel of Atlanta.

To order:

GLAD DAY BOOKS
Enfield Distribution Co.
P.O. Box 699, Enfield, NH 03748

Phone: 603-632-7377
Fax: 603-632-3611

Editorial Office
P.O. Box 112
Thetford, VT 05074

Phone: 802-785-2608

GLAD DAY BOOKS

Enfield Distribution Co.
P.O. Box 699, Enfield, NH 03748
Phone orders: 603-632-7377/888-874-6904 tollfree
Fax orders: 603-632-3611
E-mail orders: info@enfieldbooks.com

Editorial Office:
P.O. Box 112
Thetford, VT 05074
Phone: 802-785-2608

Bill to: Name: _____
Address: _____
_____
Phone: _____

Ship to: Name: _____
Address: _____
_____
Phone _____

Payment: ❐ Check or money order to GLAD DAY BOOKS is enclosed.
❐ Credit card # _____ Exp. date _____
Signature _____

TITLE/AUTHOR	ISBN	QUANTITY	PRICE
Broken Trip / Anastas	1-930180-11-x		$16.00
History and Spirit / Kovel	1-930180-08-x		$21.95
Serious Kissing / Selfridge	1-930180-00-4		$13.50
Travels in Altai / Nichols	1-930180-01-2		$16.50
Girl in Movement / Kollisch	1-930180-05-5		$16.95
Teacha! / Albarelli	1-930180-04-7		$12.95
Ecological Investigations / Morrison	1-930180-06-3		$9.95
A Voyage to New Orleans /Reclus	1-930180-12-8		$10.00
Swords / Rexroth	1-930180-02-0		$14.00
Big Bust / Gallant	1-930180-09-8		$15.00

Subtotal: _____
$4 Shipping & handling: $4.00
Additional S&H [ ] x $1.00: _____
Contribution to Glad Day Books: _____
TOTAL: _____